"Miss White—"

"Sherry!" she cried in frustration. "My name is Sherry, and this is exactly what I'm talking about. I don't call you *Mr.* Roarke, yet you insist on addressing me formally, as if I were some stiff, starched—"

"But, Sherry—"

"Thank you," she murmured, interrupting him with a soft smile. "I feel a thousand times better just having you say my name." She dropped her gaze. "I realize I haven't made things easier. And I know you've turned your head on more than one occasion while I've bent the rules."

"Bent the rules?" her repeated incredulously. "You've out-and-out pulverized them."

Sherry sighed with relief. At least he was still talking to her. Her head tilted back to question the look in his eyes. "It's important to me—no matter what happens at camp—that we always remain friends."

His brow relaxed, and a slow, sensual smile transformed his features. "Just friends?" he asked softly.

Dear Reader:

The spirit of the Silhouette Romance Homecoming Celebration lives on as each month we bring you six books by continuing stars!

And there are some wonderful stories in the stars for you. In the coming months, we're publishing romances by many of your favorite authors such as Sondra Stanford, Annette Broadrick and Brittany Young. In addition, we have some very special events planned for the summer of 1988.

In June, watch for the first book in Diana Palmer's exciting new trilogy *Long, Tall Texans*. The initial title, *Calhoun*, will be followed later by *Justin* and *Tyler*. All three books are designed to capture your heart.

Also in June is Phyllis Halldorson's *Raindance Autumn*, the second book of this wonderful author's *Raindance Duo*. Don't miss this exciting sequel!

Your response to these authors and other authors of Silhouette Romances has served as a touchstone for us, and we're pleased to bring you more books with Silhouette's distinctive medley of charm, wit and— above all—*romance*.

I hope you enjoy this book and the many stories to come. Come home to Silhouette—for always!

Sincerely,

Tara Hughes
Senior Editor
Silhouette Books

DEBBIE MACOMBER

Almost
Paradise

Silhouette *Romance*
Published by Silhouette Books New York
America's Publisher of Contemporary Romance

SILHOUETTE BOOKS
300 E. 42nd St., New York, N.Y. 10017

ISBN: 0-373-08579-6

First Silhouette Books printing May 1988

Books by Debbie Macomber

Silhouette Romance

*Legendary Lovers trilogy

Silhouette Special Edition

DEBBIE MACOMBER

has quickly become one of Silhouette's most prolific authors. As a wife and mother of four, she not only manages to keep her family happy, but she also keeps her publisher and readers happy with each book she writes.

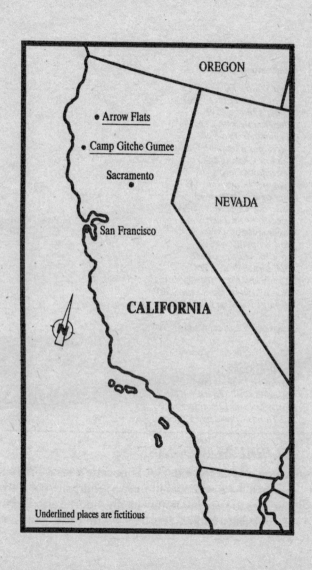

Underlined places are fictitious

Chapter One

"Mirror, mirror on the wall—who's the fairest of us all?" Sherry White propped one eye open and gazed into the small bathroom mirror. She grimaced and quickly squeezed both eyes shut. "Not me," she answered and blindly reached for her toothbrush.

Morning had never been her favorite time of day. She agreed with the old adage claiming that if God had intended people to see the sun rise, He would have caused it to happen later in the day. Unfortunately, Jeff Roarke, the director of Camp Gitche Gumee, didn't agree. He demanded his staff meet early each morning. No excuses. No reprieves. No pardons.

Fine, Sherry mused. Then he'd have to take what he got, and heaven knew she wasn't her best at this ungodly hour.

After running a brush through her long, dark curls, Sherry wrapped a scarf around her head to keep the hair away from her face and returned to her room where she reached for a sweater to ward off a chill. Then she hurried across the lush green grass of the campgrounds to the staff meeting room. Once there, a hasty glance around told her she was already late.

"Good morning, Miss White," Jeff Roarke called, when she took the last available seat.

"Morning," she mumbled under her breath, crossing her arms to disguise her embarrassment. He'd purposely called attention to her, letting the others know she was five minutes late.

His sober gaze had followed her as she'd maneuvered herself between the narrow row of chairs. Now his intense eyes remained on her until her heart hammered and indignation rose in her breast. She experienced a perverse desire to shatter Jeff Roarke's pompous attitude, but the feeling died a quiet death as she raised her gaze to meet his. Was she imagining a hint of amusement lurking there? At any rate, he was regarding her with a speculative gleam that was distinctly unsettling. Evidently satisfied that he'd unnerved her, he began to speak again.

Although she knew she should be taking notes, Sherry was having trouble tearing her gaze away from the imperious camp director, now that his attention was off her. Jeff Roarke was tall, easily over six feet, and superbly fit. His jaw was lean and well defined—okay, he was absurdly good-looking, she'd grant him that. But Sherry sensed an arrogance in him, an uncompromising authority, an aggressive virility that really got under her skin.

She'd known a month earlier when she'd met Mr. Almighty Roarke for the job interview that they weren't going to get along. She'd flown to Sacramento from Seattle and met him in his office, praying she hadn't made the long trip in vain. She'd wanted this job so badly...and then she'd blown it.

"I think it's a marvelous idea to name the camp after a cute children's song," she'd said cheerfully.

Roarke looked shocked. "Song? What song? The camp's name is taken from the poem 'Song of Hiawatha' by Henry Wadsworth Longfellow."

"Oh—uh, I mean, of course," Sherry said, her face flaming.

From there the interview seemed shaky, and Sherry was convinced she'd ruined her chances as Roarke continued to ask what seemed like a hundred questions. But although he didn't appear overly impressed with her qualifications, he handed her several forms to complete.

"You mean I'm hired?" she asked, confused. "I . . . I have the job?"

"I'd hardly have you fill out the paperwork if you didn't," he returned, his face impassive but those hazel eyes of his brimming with amusement.

"Right." Sherry's heart raced with excitement. She was going to escape her wacky stepmother, Phyliss. For one glorious summer no one need know where she was. But as Sherry began to complete the myriad forms her enthusiasm for her plan dwindled. She couldn't possibly put down references—anyone she'd list would be someone who'd have contact with her father and stepmother. The instant her family discovered where Sherry was hiding, it would be over.

Roarke seemed to note Sherry's hesitancy as she studied the forms. "Is there something you disagree with, Miss White?"

"No," she said, hurriedly filling out the names and addresses of family friends and former employers, but doing her best to make them unreadable, running the letters together and transposing numbers.

Nibbling anxiously on her bottom lip, Sherry finished and handed over the completed paperwork.

From that first meeting with Jeff Roarke, things had gone swiftly downhill. Sherry found him . . . she searched for the right word. Dictatorial, she decided. He'd let it be known as director of Camp Gitche Gumee that he expected her to abide by all the rules and regulations—which was only fair—but then he'd proceeded to give her a Michener-length manual of rules and regulations, with the understanding that she would have it read by the time camp opened. Good grief! She'd been hired as a counselor for seven little girls, not as a brain surgeon.

"Are there any questions?"

Jeff Roarke's words to the early-morning assembly broke into her consciousness, startling Sherry into the present. Worried, she glanced around her, hoping no one had noticed that she'd casually slipped into her memories.

"Most of the children will arrive today," Roarke was saying.

He'd gotten her up at this time of day to tell her that? They'd have to be a bunch of numskulls not to know when the children were coming. All week the entire staff had been working to prepare the cottages and campgrounds for the children's arrival. Sherry glared at him for all she was worth, then squirmed when he paused and stared back at her.

"Is there a problem, Miss White?"

Sherry froze as the others directed their attention to her. "N-no."

"Good—then I'll continue."

The man never smiled, Sherry mused. Not once in the past week had she seen him joke or laugh or kid around. He was like a man driven, but for what cause she could only speculate. The camp was important to him, that much she'd gleaned immediately, but why a university professor would find such purpose in a children's camp was beyond Sherry's understanding. There seemed to be an underlying sadness in Jeff Roarke, too, one that robbed his life of joy, stole the pleasure of simple things from his perception.

But none of the counselors seemed to think of Jeff Roarke the same way she did. Oh, the other female staff members certainly noticed him, Sherry admitted grudgingly. From the goo-goo eyes some of the women counselors were giving him, they too were impressed with his dark good looks. But he was so stiff, so dry, so serious that Sherry considered him a lost cause. And she had enough on her mind without complicating her life worrying about someone like the camp director.

Sherry expected to have fun this summer. She needed it. The last three years of college, living near home, had left her mentally drained and physically exhausted. School was only partly to blame for her condition. Phyliss was responsible for the rest. Phyliss and her father had married when Sherry was a college freshman and Phyliss, bless her heart, had never had children. Seeing Sherry as her one and only opportunity to be a mother, she'd attacked the project with such gusto that Sherry was still reeling from the effects three years later. Phyliss worried that Sherry wasn't eating well enough. Phyliss worried about the hours she kept. Phyliss worried that she studied too hard. To state the problem simply—Phyliss worried.

As a dedicated health nut, her stepmother made certain that Sherry ate correctly. There were days Sherry would have killed for a pizza or a hot dog, but Phyliss wouldn't hear of it. Then there was the matter of clothes. Phyliss loved bright colors—and so did Sherry, in moderation.

Unfortunately, her stepmother considered it her duty to shop with Sherry and "help" her choose the proper clothes for college. As a result, her closet was full of purples, army greens, sunshine yellows and hot, sizzling pinks.

So she'd planned this summer as an escape from her wonderful but wacky stepmother. Sherry wasn't exactly proud of the way she'd slipped away in the middle of the night, but she'd thought it best to avoid the multitude of questions Phyliss would ply her with had she known Sherry was leaving. She'd managed to escape with a note mailed from the airport that stated in vague terms that she was going to camp for the summer. She hated to be so under-handed, but knowing Phyliss, the woman would arrive with a new wardrobe of coordinated shades of char-treuse—and order Sherry's meals catered when she learned that her beloved stepdaughter was eating camp food.

Sherry had chosen Camp Gitche Gumee because it had intrigued her. Being counselor to a group of intellectually gifted children in the heart of the majestic California red-woods sounded like the perfect escape. And Phyliss would never think to search California.

"Within the next few hours, fifty children will be arriv-ing from all around the country," Roarke continued.

Sherry childishly rolled her eyes toward the ceiling. He could just as well have given them this information at seven—the birds weren't even awake yet! Expecting her to retain vital information at this unreasonable hour was going beyond the call of duty.

"Each cottage will house seven children; Fred Spen-cer's cabin will house eight. Counselors, see me following the meeting for the names of your charges. Wherever pos-sible, I've attempted to match the child with a friend in an effort to cut down on homesickness."

That made sense to Sherry, but little else did.

As Roarke continued speaking, Sherry's thoughts drifted again. In addition to Jeff Roarke, their fearless leader, Sherry knew she was going to have problems getting along with Fred Spencer, who was counselor for the nine- and ten-year-old boys. Fred had been a counselor at Camp Gitche Gumee for several summers and was solidly set in the way he handled his charges.

Sherry had come up with some ideas she'd wanted to talk over in the first few days following her arrival. Since Fred was the counselor for the same age group as hers, it had seemed natural to go to him. But Fred had found a reason to reject every suggestion. Five minutes with him and Sherry discovered that he didn't possess a creative bone in his body and frowned dutifully upon anyone who deviated from the norm. But more than disagreeing with her, Sherry had gotten the impression that Fred highly disapproved of her. She wasn't sure what she'd done to invoke his ire, but his resentment toward her was strong enough to cause her to feel uneasy whenever they were in the room together.

With a sigh, Sherry forced her attention back to Roarke. He continued speaking for several minutes, but most of what he had to say was directed to the housekeepers, cooks and grounds keepers. The classroom teachers had been briefed the day before.

A half hour later the staff was dismissed for breakfast—and not a minute too soon, Sherry mused as she walked toward the large dining hall. Blindly she headed for the coffeepot. If Jeff Roarke was going to call staff meetings when the moon was still out, the least he could do was provide coffee.

"Miss White," Roarke called, stopping her.

Sherry glanced longingly toward the coffeepot. "Yes?"

"Could I speak to you a minute?"

"Sure." She headed toward the back of the dining hall, where he was waiting for her.

Roarke watched the newest staff member of Camp Gitche Gumee make her way toward him, walking between the long tables, and he smiled inwardly. That Sherry White wasn't a morning person was obvious. During the staff meeting, her eyes had drooped half-closed and she'd stifled more than one yawn. For part of that time her features had been frozen into a far-away look, as though she were caught in some daydream.

Thinking about her, Roarke felt his brow crease into a slight frown. He'd hired her on impulse, something he rarely acted upon. He'd liked her smile and her spirit and had gotten a chuckle out of her misunderstanding about the name of the camp. He found her appealing, yet she made him nervous, too, in a way he couldn't explain even to himself. All he knew was that she'd shown up for the interview, and before he'd realized what he was doing, he'd hired her. In analyzing his actions later, Roarke had been astonished. Liking the way she smiled and the way her eyes softened when she spoke of children were not good enough reasons to hire her as a counselor. Yet he felt he hadn't made an impossible choice. In spite of her apparent dislike of his methods, Roarke felt she would do an excellent job with the children, and more than a good personality match with him, the youngsters were what was most important.

"Yes?" Sherry asked, joining him. Her gaze remained a little too obviously on the coffeepot on the other side of the room.

Opening his briefcase, Roarke withdrew a camp reference sheet and handed it to her. "I'm sorry to bother you, but your application form must have gotten smeared across the top—I wasn't able to read the names of your references."

Sherry swallowed uncomfortably. She should have known scribbled letters and numbers wouldn't work.

"Could you fill this out and have it back to me later this afternoon?"

"Sure—no problem," she said, her smile forced.

"Well," he said, puzzled by the frown that worried her brow, "I'll see you later, then."

"Later," she agreed distractedly. Her gaze fell to the form. If worst came to worst she could always give him false telephone numbers and phony addresses. But that could lead to future problems. Of course if she didn't, it could lead to problems right now!

Depressed, Sherry folded the form, then made a beeline for the coffee. Claiming her seat, she propped her elbows on the table and held the thick ceramic mug with both hands, letting the aroma stir her senses to life. She might not function well in the mornings, but she'd manage for this one summer. She'd have to if Roarke intended to keep holding these merciless 5:00 a.m. staff meetings.

"Morning," Lynn Duffy called out as she approached. Lynn, who had been assigned as housekeeper to Sherry's cabin, claimed the chair next to Sherry's. She set her tray on the table and unloaded her plate, which was heaped with scrambled eggs, bacon and toast. "Aren't you eating?"

Sherry shook her head. "Not this morning."

"Hey, this camp has a reputation for wonderful food."

"I'm not hungry. Thanks anyway." Sherry rested her chin in her hands, worrying about the references and what she could put down that would satisfy Jeff Roarke. "I wonder what kind of stupid rule he's going to come up with next," she muttered, setting the paper beside her mug.

"Jeff Roarke?"

"Yes, Roarke." Somehow Sherry couldn't think of the camp director as "Jeff." She associated that name with someone who was kind and considerate, like Lassie's owner or an affectionate uncle.

"You have to admit he's got a grip on matters."

"Sure," Sherry admitted reluctantly. Roarke ran this camp with the efficiency of a Marine boot camp. "But I have yet to see a hint of originality. For instance, I can't imagine children's cottages named Cabin One, Cabin Two and so on."

"It's less confusing that way."

"These kids are supposed to be geniuses, I strongly suspect they could keep track of a real name as easily as a boring, unadorned number."

"Maybe so," Lynn said and shook her head. "No one's ever said anything before."

"But surely the other counselors have offered suggestions."

"Not that I've heard."

Sherry raised her eyebrows. "I'd have thought the staff would want something more creative than numbers for their cabins."

"I'm sure Mr. Roarke thought the kids would be more comfortable with numbers. Several of the children are said to be mathematical wizards."

"I suppose," Sherry agreed. Roarke was totally committed to the children and the camp—Sherry didn't question that—but to her way of thinking his intentions were misdirected. Every part of camp life was geared toward academia, with little emphasis, from what she could see, on fun and games.

Lynn's deep blue eyes took on a dreamy look. She shook her head. "I think the whole idea of a special camp like this is such a good one. From what I understand, Mr. Roarke is solely responsible for organizing it. He worked years for these summer sessions. For the past four summers, he hasn't taken a penny for all his efforts. He does it for the kids.''

The news surprised Sherry, and she found herself revising her opinion of the camp director once again. The man intrigued her, she had to admit. He angered and confused her, but he fascinated her, too. Sherry didn't know what to think anymore. If only he weren't such a stick-in-the-mud. She remembered that Lynn was one of those who had been making sheep's eyes at Roarke earlier. "I have the feeling you think Jeff Roarke is wonderful," she suggested.

Lynn nodded and released a heavy sigh. "Does it show that much?"

"Not really."

"He's so handsome," Lynn continued. "Surely you've noticed?"

Sherry took another sip of her coffee to delay answering. "I suppose."

"And so successful. Rumors flew around here last summer when Mr. Roarke became the head of the economics department for Cal Tech."

Again Sherry paid close attention to her coffee. "I'm impressed."

"From what I understand he's written a book."

A smile touched the corners of Sherry's mouth. She could well imagine what dry reading anything Roarke had written would be.

"Apparently his book caused quite a stir in Washington. The director of the Federal Reserve recommended it to the President."

"Wow!" Sherry was impressed.

"And he's handsome to boot."

"That much is fairly obvious," Sherry allowed. All right, Jeff Roarke was lean and muscular with eyes that could make a woman go all soft inside, but she wasn't the only one to have noticed that, and she certainly wasn't interested in becoming a groupie.

"He really gets to me," Lynn said with a sigh.

"He does have nice eyes," Sherry admitted reluctantly.

Lynn nodded and continued. "They're so unusual. Yesterday when we were talking I would have sworn they were green, but when I first met him they were an incredible hazel color."

"I guess I hadn't noticed," Sherry commented. Okay, so she lied!

Carefully Lynn set her fork beside her plate, her look thoughtful. "You don't like him much, do you?"

"Oh, I like him—it's just that I figured a camp for children would be fun. This place is going to be about as lively as a prison. There are classes scheduled day and night. From the look of things, all the kids are going to do is study. There isn't any time left for fun."

Evidently Lynn found her observations humorous. A smile created twin dimples in her smooth cheeks. "Just wait until the kids get here. Then you'll be grateful for Mr. Roarke's high sense of order."

Maybe so, Sherry thought, but that remained to be seen. "You worked here last summer?"

Lynn nodded as she swallowed a mouthful of eggs. "I was a housekeeper then, too. Several of us are back for a second go-around, but Mr. Roarke's the real reason I came back." She hesitated. "How old do you think he is?"

"Roarke? I don't know. Close to thirty, I'd guess."

"Oh dear, that's probably much too old for someone nineteen."

Lynn's look of abject misery caused Sherry to laugh outright. "I've heard of greater age differences."

"How old are you?"

"Twenty-one," Sherry answered.

Lynn wrinkled her nose, as though she envied Sherry those years. "Don't get me wrong. There's no chance of a romance developing between Mr. Roarke and me, or me and anyone else for that matter—at least not until camp is dismissed."

"Why not?"

"Mr. Roarke is death on camp romances," Lynn explained. "Last year two of the counselors fell in love, and when Mr. Roarke found them kissing he threatened to dismiss them both." Lynn sighed expressively and a dreamy look came over her. "You know what I think?"

Sherry could only speculate. "What?"

"I think Mr. Roarke's been burned. His tender heart was shattered by a careless affair that left him bleeding and raw. And now—years later—he's afraid to love again, afraid to offer his heart to another woman." Dramatically, Lynn placed her hand over her own heart as though to protect it from the fate of love turned sour. She gazed somberly into the distance.

The strains of a Righteous Brothers song hummed softly in the distance, and it was all Sherry could do to swallow down a laugh. "You know this for a fact?"

"Heavens, no. That's just what I think must have happened to him. It makes sense, doesn't it?"

"Ah—I'm not sure." Sherry hedged.

"Mr. Roarke is really against camp romances. You should have been here last year. I don't think I've ever seen him more upset. He claimed romance and camp just don't mix."

"He's right about that." To find herself agreeing with Roarke was a surprise, but Sherry could see the pitfalls of a group of counselors more interested in one another than in their charges.

Lynn shrugged again. "I don't think there's anything wrong with a light flirtation, but Mr. Roarke has other ideas. There are even rules and regulations on how male and female counselors should behave in each other's company. But I suppose you've already read that."

When Sherry didn't respond, Lynn eyed her speculatively. "You did read the manual, didn't you?"

Sherry dropped her gaze to the tabletop. "Sort of."

"You'd better, because if he catches you going against the rules, your neck will be on the chopping block."

A lump developed in Sherry's throat as she remembered the problem with her references. She'd need to keep a low profile. And from the sound of things, she had best be a good little counselor and keep her opinions to herself. What Lynn had said about studying the manual made sense. Sherry vowed inwardly to read it all the way through and do her utmost to follow the rules, no matter what she thought.

"You'll do fine," Lynn said confidently. "And the kids are going to really like you."

"I hope so." Unexpected doubts were jumping up and down inside Sherry like youngsters on pogo sticks. She had thought she'd be a natural for this position. Her major was education, and with her flair for originality, she hoped to be a good teacher. The kids she'd come here to counsel weren't everyday run-of-the-mill nine- and ten-year-olds, they were bona fide geniuses. Each child had an IQ in the ninety-eight percentile. She lifted her chin in sudden determination. She'd always appreciated a challenge. She'd been looking forward to this summer, and she wasn't about to let Jeff Roarke and his rules and regulations ruin it for her.

"The only time you need to worry is if Mr. Roarke calls you to his office after breakfast," Lynn said, interrupting Sherry's thoughts.

Sherry digested this information. "Why then?"

Lynn paused long enough to peel back the aluminum tab on a small container of strawberry jam. "The only time anyone is ever fired is in the morning. The couple I mentioned earlier, who fell in love last summer—their names were Sue and Mark—they talked to Mr. Roarke on three separate occasions. Each time in the afternoon. Every time Sue heard her name read from the daily bulletin she became a nervous wreck until she heard the time of the scheduled meeting. Mark didn't fare much better. They both expected to get the ax at any minute."

"Roarke didn't fire them?"

"No, but he threatened to. They weren't even allowed to hold hands."

"I bet they were miserable." Sherry could sympathize with both sides. She was young enough to appreciate the temptations of wanting to be with a boy at camp but old enough to recognize the pitfalls of such a romance.

"But worse than a camp romance, Mr. Roarke is a stickler for honesty. He won't tolerate anyone who so much as stretches the truth."

"Really?" Sherry murmured. Suddenly swallowing became difficult.

"Last year a guy came to camp who fibbed about his age. He was one of three Mr. Roarke fired. It's true Danny had lied, but only by a few months. He was out of here so fast it made my head spin. Of course, he got called in to Roarke's office in the morning," she added.

"My goodness." Sherry's mouth had gone dry. If Roarke decided to check her references her days at Camp Gitche Gumee were surely numbered.

"Well, I'd best go plug in my vacuum."

"Yeah—" Sherry raised her hand "—I'll talk to you later."

The younger girl stood and scooted her chair back into position. "Good luck."

Sherry watched the lanky teenager leave the mess hall, and for the first time she considered that maybe escaping Phyliss at summer camp hadn't been such a brilliant idea after all.

Chapter Two

Three hours later the first bus load of children pulled into Camp Gitche Gumee. The bus was from nearby Sacramento and the surrounding area, but Roarke had announced at their morning get-together that there were children traveling from as far away as Maine and Vermont. The sum these parents paid for two months of camp had shocked Sherry, but who was she to quibble? She had a summer job, and in spite of her misgivings about the camp director, she was pleased to be here.

Standing inside her cabin, Sherry breathed in the clean scent of the forest and waited anxiously for her charges to be escorted to her cabin. When she chanced a peek out the door, she noted Peter Towne, the camp lifeguard, leading a forlorn-looking girl with long, dark braids toward her.

Sherry stepped onto the porch to meet the pair. She tried to get the little girl to meet her gaze so she could smile at her, but the youngster seemed determined to study the grass.

"Miss White, this is Pamela Reynolds."

"Hello, Pamela."

"Hi."

Peter handed Sherry Pamela's suitcase.

Thanking him with a smile, Sherry placed her free hand on the shy girl's shoulder and led her into the cabin.

The youngster's eyes narrowed suspiciously as she sat on the nearest bunk. "You're not scared of animals are you?"

"Nope." That wasn't entirely true, but Sherry didn't consider it a good idea to let any of her charges know she wasn't especially fond of snakes. Not when the woods were ripe for the picking.

"Good."

"Good?" Sherry repeated suspiciously.

With a nervous movement, Pamela nodded, placed her suitcase on the thin mattress and opened it. From inside, she lifted a shoe box with holes punched in the top. "I brought along my hamster. I can keep him, can't I?" Blue eyes pleaded with her.

Sherry didn't know what to say. According to the camp manual, pets weren't allowed. But a hamster wasn't like a dog or a cat or a horse, for heaven's sake. Sherry hedged. "What's his name?"

"Ralph."

"That's a nice name." Her brain was frantically working.

"He won't make any noise and he barely eats anything and I couldn't leave him at home because my parents are going to Europe and I know we aren't supposed to bring along animals, but Ralph is the very best friend I have and I'd miss him too much if he had to stay with Mrs. Murphy like my little brother."

Appealing tears glistened in the little girl's eyes and Sherry felt herself weaken. It shouldn't be that difficult to keep one tiny hamster from Roarke's attention.

"But will Ralph be happy living in a cabin full of girls?"

"Oh, sure," Pam said, the words rushing out, "he likes girls, and he's really a wonderful hamster. Do you want to hold him?"

"No thanks," Sherry answered brightly. The manual might have a full page dedicated to pets, but it didn't say anything about adopting a mascot. "If the others agree, I feel we can keep Ralph as our mascot—as long as we don't let any of the other cabins find out about him." Sherry cringed inwardly at the thought of Jeff Roarke's reaction to her decision. The thought of his finding a pet, even something as unobtrusive as a hamster, wasn't a pleasant one, but from the looks of it the little girl was strongly attached to the rodent. Housing Ralph seemed such a little thing to keep a child happy. Surely what Ironjaw didn't know wouldn't hurt him....

Three ten-year-olds, Sally, Wendy and Diane, were escorted to the cabin when the next bus load arrived. Although they were different in looks and size, the three shared a serious, somber nature. Sherry had expected rambunctious children. Instead, she had been assigned miniature adults.

Sally had brought along her microscope and several specimens she planned to examine before dinner. Sherry didn't ask to see them, but from the contents of the jars that lined Sally's headboard, she didn't want to know what the child planned to study. Sherry's social circle didn't include many nine- and ten-year-olds, but she wasn't acquainted with a single child who kept pig embryos in jars of formaldehyde as companions.

Wendy, at least, appeared to be a halfway normal pre-teen. She collected dolls and had brought along an assortment of her prize Barbies and Kens, including designer outfits for each. She arranged them across the head of her bed and introduced Sherry to Barbie-Samantha, Barbie-Jana and Barbie-Brenda. The Kens were also distinguished with their own names, and by the time Wendy had finished, Sherry's head was swimming.

Sherry didn't know what to make of Diane. The ten-year-old barely said a word. She chose her bunk, unpacked and then immediately started to read. Sherry noted that Diane's suitcases contained a bare minimum of clothes and were filled to capacity with books. Scanning the academic titles caused Sherry to grimace; she didn't see a single Nancy Drew.

Twins, Jan and Jill, were the next to make their entrance. They were blond replicas of each other and impossible to tell apart until they smiled. Jan was lacking both upper front teeth. Jill was lacking only one. Sherry felt a little smug until she discovered Jill wiggling her lone front tooth back and forth in an effort to extract it. Before the day was over, Sherry realized, she would be at their mercy. Fine, she decided, the two knew who they were—she'd let them sort it out.

The last child assigned to Cabin Four was Gretchen. Sherry recognized the minute the ten-year-old showed up that this child was trouble.

"This camp gets dumpier every summer," Gretchen grumbled, folding her arms around her middle as she surveyed the cabin. She paused and glanced at the last remaining cot. "I refuse to sleep near the window. I'll get a nosebleed and a headache if I'm near a breeze."

"Okay," Sherry said. "Is there anyone here who would like to trade with Gretchen?"

Pam suddenly found it necessary to feed Ralph.

Sally brought out her microscope.

Wendy twisted Barbie-Brenda into Ken-Brian's arms and placed them in a position Sherry preferred not to question. Soon, no fewer than three Barbies and an equal number of Kens were in a tangled mess of arms and legs.

Jan and Jill sat on the end of their bunks staring blindly into space while Jill worked furiously on extracting her front tooth.

Diane kept a book of mathematical brainteasers propped open in front of her face and didn't give any indication that she'd heard the request.

"It doesn't look like anyone wants to trade," Sherry told the youngster, whose mouth was twisted with a sour look. "Since you've been to camp before, you knew that the first to arrive claim the beds they want. I saw you lingering outside earlier this afternoon. You should have checked in here first."

"I refuse to sleep near the window," Gretchen announced for the second time.

"In that case, I'll place the mattress on the floor in my room and you can bunk there, although I feel you should know, I sometimes sleep with my window open."

"I sincerely hope you're teasing," Gretchen returned, eyes wide and incredulous. "There are things crawling around down there." She studiously pointed to the wood floor.

"Where?" Sally cried, immediately interested. Her hand curled around the base of her microscope.

"I believe she was speaking hypothetically," Sherry mumbled.

"Oh."

"All right, I'll sleep by the window and ignore the medical risk," Gretchen said heatedly. She carelessly tossed her suitcase on top of the mattress. "But I'm writing my mother and telling her about this. She's paying good money for me to attend this camp and she expects me to receive the very best of care. There's no excuse for me to be mistreated in this manner."

"Let's see how it goes, shall we?" Sherry suggested, biting her tongue. This kid was a medical risk all right, but the only thing in danger was Sherry's mental health. Already she could feel a pounding headache coming on. By sheer force of will, she managed to keep her fingers from massaging her temples. First Roarke and now Gretchen. No doubt they were related.

"My uncle is a congressman," Gretchen said, to no one in particular. "I may write him instead."

The entire cabin pretended not to hear, which only seemed to infuriate Gretchen. She paused smugly. "Is Mr. Roarke the camp director again this year?"

"Yes," Sherry answered cheerfully. She knew it! Roarke was most likely another of this pest's uncles. "Would you like me to make an appointment for you to speak to him?"

"Yes. I'll let him handle this unfortunate situation." Gretchen removed her suitcase from the bunk and gingerly set it aside, seemingly assured that the camp director would assign her a cot anywhere she wanted.

"I'll see if I can arrange it when you're in the computer class," Sherry said.

By afternoon Camp Gitche Gumee was in full swing. Cabins were filled to capacity and the clamor of children sounded throughout the compound.

After the girls had unpacked and stored their luggage, Sherry led them into the dining hall. Counselors were expected to eat their meals with their charges, but after lunch Sherry's time was basically free. On occasion she would be given the opportunity to schedule outdoor activities such as canoeing and hiking expeditions, but those were left for her to organize. Most of the camp was centered around challenging academic pursuits. Sessions were offered in biochemistry, computer skills and propositional calculus. Sherry wondered what ever happened to stringing beads and basket weaving!

When the girls were dismissed for their afternoon activities, Sherry made her way to the director's office, which was on the other side of the campgrounds, far from the maddening crowd, she noted. It was all too apparent that Roarke liked his privacy.

Tall redwoods outlined the camp outskirts. Wildflowers grew in abundance. Goldthreads, red baneberry and the northern inside-out flower were just a few that Sherry recognized readily. She had a passion for wildflowers and could name those most common to the West Coast. Some flowers were unknown to her, but she had a sneaky suspicion that if she picked a few, either Sally or Diane would be able to tell her the species and Latin title.

When she could delay the inevitable no longer, Sherry approached Roarke's office. She knocked politely twice and waited.

"Come in," came the gruff voice.

Squaring her shoulders, preparing to face the lion in his den, Sherry entered the office. As she expected, his room was meticulously neat. Bookshelves lined the walls, and where there weren't books the space was covered with certificates. His desk was an oversize mahogany one that rested in the center of the large room. The leather highbacked chair was one Sherry would have expected to find a bank president using—not a camp director.

"Miss White."

"Mr. Roarke."

They greeted each other stiffly.

"Sit down." He motioned toward the two low-backed upholstered chairs.

Sherry sat and briefly studied the man behind the desk. He looked to be a young thirty although there were lines faintly etched around his eyes and on both sides of his mouth. But instead of detracting from his good looks, the lines added another dimension to his appeal. Lynn's words about Roarke suffering from a lost love played back in Sherry's mind. Again she sensed an underlying sadness in him, but nothing that could readily be seen in the square, determined lines of his jaw. And again it was his piercing gaze that captured her.

"You brought back the reference sheet?" Roarke prompted.

"Yes." Sherry sat at the edge of her seat as though she expected to blurt out what she had to say and make a mad dash for the door. She'd reprinted the names and addresses more clearly this time, transposing the numbers and hoping that it would look unintentional when the letters were delayed.

"I have it with me," she answered, and set the form on his desk. "But there's something else I'd like to discuss. I've been assigned Gretchen Hamburg."

"Ah, yes, Gretchen."

Apparently the girl was known to him. "I'm afraid I'm having a small problem with her," Sherry said, carefully choosing her words. "It seems Gretchen prefers to sleep away from the window, but she dawdled around outside while the others chose bunks, and now she's complaining. She's asked that I make an appointment for her to plead her case with you. She...insinuated that you'd correct this situation for her."

"I'm—"

Sherry didn't allow him to finish. "It's my opinion that giving in to Gretchen's demands would set a precedent that would cause problems among the other girls later."

His wide brow furrowed. "I can understand your concerns."

Sherry relaxed, scooting back in her chair.

"However, Gretchen's family is an influential one."

Sherry bolted forward. "That's favoritism."

"Won't any of the other girls trade with her?"

"I've already suggested that. But the others shouldn't be forced into giving up their beds simply because Gretchen Hamburg—"

"Have you sought a compromise?" he interrupted.

Sherry's hands were clenched in such tight fists that her punch would have challenged Muhammad Ali's powerful right hand. "I suggested that we place the mattress on the floor in my room, but I did mention that I sometimes sleep with my window open."

"And?"

"And Gretchen insisted on speaking to you personally."

Roarke drummed his fingers on the desktop. "If you haven't already noticed, Gretchen is a complainer."

"No!" Sherry feigned wide-eyed shock.

Roarke studied the fiery flash in Sherry's dark brown eyes and again experienced an unfamiliar tug on his emotions. She made him want to laugh at the most inappropriate times. And when he wasn't amused by her, she infuriated him. There didn't seem to be any in-between in the emotions he felt for her. Sherry White could be a problem, Roarke mused, although he was convinced she'd be a terrific counselor. The trouble was within himself. He was attracted to her—strongly. He would have been better off not to have hired her than to wage battle with his emotions all summer. He'd need to keep a cool head with her—keep his distance, avoid her whenever possible, bury whatever it was in her that he found so appealing.

Sherry was convinced she saw a brief smile touch Roarke's mouth, so faint that it was gone before it completely registered with her. If only he'd really smile or joke or kid, she would find it infinitely more pleasant to meet with him. A lock of hair fell across his brow and he brushed it back only to have it immediately return to its former position. Sherry found her gaze mesmerized by that single lock. Except for those few strands of cocky hair Roarke was impeccable in every way. She sincerely doubted that as a child his jeans had ever been torn or grass stained.

"Well?" Sherry prompted. "Should I send Gretchen in to see you?"

"No."

"No?"

"That's what I said, Miss White. I can't be bothered with these minor details. Handle the situation as you see fit."

Using the arms of the chair for leverage, Sherry rose. She was pleased because she didn't want Ms. Miserable to use Roarke to manipulate her and the other girls in the cabin. Sherry was halfway out the door when Roarke spoke next.

"However, if this matter isn't settled promptly, I'll be forced to handle the situation myself. Dorothy Hamburg has been a faithful supporter of this camp for several years."

Well, she might as well jerk Pamela and Ralph from the center cot, Sherry thought irritably. One way or another Gretchen was bound to have her own way.

Chapter Three

Dressed in their pajamas, the seven preteens sat Indian fashion on their cots, listening wide-eyed and intent as Sherry read.

"And they lived happily ever after," Sherry murmured, slowly closing the large book.

"You don't really believe that garbage, do you?" Gretchen demanded.

Sherry smiled softly to herself. Gretchen found fault with everything, she'd discovered over the course of the first week of camp. Even when the little girl enjoyed something, it was her nature to complain, quibble and frown. During the fairy tale, Gretchen had been the child most enraptured, yet she seemed to feel it was her duty to nitpick.

"How do you mean?" Sherry asked, deciding to play innocent. The proud tilt of Gretchen's chin tore at her heart.

"It's only a stupid fairy tale."

"But it was so lovely," Wendy chimed in softly.

"And the Prince..."

"...was so handsome." Jan and Jill added in unison.

"But none of it is true." Gretchen crossed her arms and pressed her lips tightly together. "My mother claims that she's suffering from the Cinderella syndrome, and here you are telling us the same goofy story and expecting us to believe it."

"Oh no," Sherry whispered, bending forward as though to share a special secret. "Fairy tales don't have to be true; but it's romantic to pretend. That's what makes them so special."

"But fairy tales couldn't possibly be real."

"All fiction is make-believe," Sherry softly assured her chronic complainer.

"I don't care if it's true or not, I like it when you read us stories," Diane volunteered. The child had set aside Proust in favor of listening to the bedtime story. Sherry felt a sense of pride that she'd been able to interest Diane in something beyond the heavy reading material she devoured at all hours of the night and day.

"Tell us another one," Wendy begged. Her Barbie and Ken dolls sat in a circle in front of her, their arms twisting around one another.

Sherry closed the book. "I will tomorrow night."

"Another fairy tale, okay?" Pamela insisted. "Even though he's a boy, Ralph liked it." She petted the hamster and reverently kissed him good-night before placing him back inside his shoe-box home.

Sherry had serious doubts about Ralph's environment, but Pamela had repeatedly assured her that the box was the only home Ralph had ever known and that he'd never run away. All the time the child spent grooming and training him lent Sherry confidence. But then, she hadn't known that many trick hamsters in her time.

"Will you read *Snow White and the Seven Dwarfs* next?" Sally wanted to know. She climbed into her cot and tucked the microscope underneath her pillow.

"Snow White it is."

"You're sort of like Snow White, aren't you?" Diane asked. "I mean, your name is White and you live in a cottage in the forest with seven dwarfs."

"Yeah!" Jan and Jill chimed together.

"I, for one, resent being referred to as a dwarf," Gretchen muttered.

"Wizards then," Wendy offered. "We're all smart."

"Snow White and the Seven Wizards," Sally commented, obviously pleased with herself. "Hey, we all live in Snow White's cottage."

"Right!" Jan and Jill said, with identical nods.

"But who's Prince Charming?"

"I don't think that this particular Snow White has a Prince Charming," Sherry said, feigning a sad sigh. "But—" she pointed her index finger toward the ceiling "—some day my prince will come."

"Mr. Roarke," Gretchen piped in excitedly. "He's the handsomest, noblest, nicest man I know. He'll be your prince."

Sherry nearly swallowed her tongue in her rush to disagree. Jeff Roarke! Impossible! He was more like the evil huntsman intent on doing away with the unsuspecting Snow White. If he ever checked her references, doing away with her would be exactly what happened! In the past week, Sherry had done her utmost to be the most accommodating counselor at camp. She hadn't given Roarke a single reason to notice or disapprove of her. Other than an

occasional gruff hello, she'd been able to avoid speaking
to him.

"Lights out everyone," Sherry said, determined to kill
the conversation before it got out of hand. The less said
about Roarke as Prince Charming, the better. The girls
were much too young to understand that to be called
princely a man must possess certain character traits. Sherry
hesitated and drew in a shaky breath. All right, she'd admit it—Jeff Roarke's character was sterling. He was dedicated, hardworking and seemed to genuinely love the
children. And then there were those incredible eyes of his.
Sherry sharply shook herself back into reality. A single
week with her charges and already she was going bongos.
Roarke was much too dictatorial and inflexible to be a
prince. At least to be *her* Prince Charming.

With a flip of the switch the room went dark. The only
illumination was a shallow path of golden moonlight
across the polished wood of the cabin floor.

Sherry moved into her own room and left the door ajar
in order to hear her seven wizards in case of bad dreams or
nighttime troubles. The girls never ceased to surprise her.
It was as though they didn't realize they were children.
When Sherry suggested reading a fairy tale, they'd moaned
and claimed that was *kids'* stuff! Sherry had persisted, and
now she was exceptionally pleased that she had. They'd
loved *Cinderella* and eaten up *Little Red Riding Hood*.
Diane, the reader, who had teethed on Ibsen, Maupassant
and Emerson, wasn't sure who the Brothers Grimm were.
But she sat night after night, her hands cupping her face
as she listened to a different type of classic—and loved it.

Sally, at ten, knew more about biochemistry than Sherry
ever hoped to understand in her lifetime. Yet Sally couldn't
name a single record in the top ten and hadn't thought to

bring a radio to camp. Her microscope was far more important!

These little geniuses were still children, and if no one else was going to remind them of that fact, Sherry was! If she could, she would have liked to scream that in Jeff Roarke's face. He had to realize there was more to life than academia; yet the entire camp seemed centered around challenging the mind and leaving the heart empty.

Sitting on the edge of her cot, Sherry's gaze fell on the seven girls in the room outside her own. She had been given charge of these little ones for the next two months, and by golly she was going to teach these children to have fun if it killed her!

"Ralph!"

The shrill cry pierced Sherry's peaceful slumber. She managed to open one eye and peek toward the clock radio. Four-thirteen. She had a full seventeen minutes before her alarm was set to ring.

"Miss White," Pamela cried, frantically stumbling into Sherry's room. "Ralph is gone!"

"What!" Holding a sheet to her breast, Sherry jerked upright, eyes wide. "Gone? What do you mean gone?"

"He's run away," the little girl sobbed. "I woke up and found the lid from the shoe box off kilter, and when I looked he was...m-missing." She burst into tears and threw her arms around Sherry's neck, weeping pathetically.

"He didn't run away," Sherry said, thinking fast as she hugged the thin child.

"He didn't?" Pamela raised her tear-streaked face and battled down a fresh wave of emotion. "Then where is he?"

"He's exploring. Remember what I said about Ralph getting tired of his shoe-box home? He just went on an adventure into the woods to find some friends."

Pamela nodded, her dark braids bouncing.

"I suppose he woke up in the middle of the night and decided that he'd like to see who else was living around the cabin." The thought was a chilling one to Sherry. She squelched it quickly.

"But where is he?"

"I...I'm not exactly sure. He may need some guidance finding his way home."

"Then we should help him."

"Right." Stretching across the bed, Sherry turned on the bedside lamp. "Ralph," she called softly. "Allie, allie oxen free." It wouldn't be that easy, but it was worth a shot.

"There he is," Sally cried, sitting up in her cot. She pointed to the dresser on the far side of the outer room. "He ran under there."

"Get him," Pamela screamed and raced out of Sherry's quarters.

Soon all seven girls were crawling around the floor in their long flannel nightgowns looking for Ralph. He was still at large when Sherry's alarm clock buzzed.

"Damn," she muttered under her breath. She looked up to find seven pairs of eyes accusing her. "I mean darn," she muttered back. The search party returned to their rescue mission.

"I've got to get to the staff meeting," Sherry announced dejectedly five minutes later when Ginny, the high-school girl who was working in hopes of being hired as a counselor next summer, arrived to replace her. "Listen, don't say a word to anyone about Ralph. I'll be back as quickly as I can."

"Okay," Jan and Jill answered for the group.

Because she knew what Roarke would say once she asked him about the hamster, Sherry had yet to mention Ralph's presence in their happy little cabin. To be honest, she hadn't figured on doing so. However, having the entire cabin turned upside down in an effort to locate the Dr. Livingstone of the animal kingdom was another matter.

Dressing as quickly as possible, Sherry hopped around on one foot in an effort to tie her shoelace, then switched legs and continued hopping across her pine floor.

"That's working," Diane cried, glancing in Sherry's direction. "Keep doing it."

"I see him. I see him. Ralph, come home. Ralph come home," Pamela begged, charging in the flannel night-gown over the cold floor.

A minute later, Sherry was out the door, leaving her charges to the mercy of one fickle-hearted hamster. By the time she reached the staff meeting she was panting and breathless. Roarke had already opened the meeting, and when Sherry entered, he paused and waited for her to take a seat.

"I'm pleased you saw fit to join us, Miss White," Roarke commented coolly.

"Sorry. I overslept," she mumbled as she claimed the last available chair in the front row. Rich color blossomed in her already flushed cheeks, reminding her once again why she'd come to dislike Jeff Roarke. The man went out of his way to cause her embarrassment—seemed to thrive on it.

Roarke read the list of activities for the day, listing possible educational ventures for each cabin's nightly get-togethers. Then, by turn, he had the counselors tell the others how they'd chosen to close another camping day.

"We discussed how to split an atom," the first counselor, a college freshman, told the group.

This appeared to please Roarke. "Excellent," he said, nodding his head approvingly.

"We dissected a frog," the second counselor added.

As each spoke, Sherry grew more uncomfortable. The neckline of her thin sweater felt exceptionally tight, and when it was her turn, her voice came out sounding thin and low. "I read them the Cinderella story," she said.

"Excuse me." Roarke took a step closer. "Would you kindly repeat that?"

"Yes, of course." Sherry paused and cleared her throat. "I read my girls 'Cinderella.'"

A needle dropping against the floor would have sounded like a sonic boom in the thick silence that followed.

"Cinderella," Roarke repeated, as though he was convinced he hadn't heard her correctly.

"That's right."

"Perhaps she could explain why anyone would choose to read a useless fairy tale over a worthwhile learning experience?"

The voice behind Sherry was familiar. She turned to find Fred Spencer glaring at her with undisguised disapproval. Since their first disagreement over Sherry's ideas, they hadn't exchanged more than a few words.

Sherry turned her head around and tucked her hands under her thighs, shifting her weight back and forth over her knuckles. "I consider fairy tales a valuable learning tool."

"You do?" This time it was Roarke who questioned her.

From the way he was looking at her, Sherry could tell that he was having a difficult time accepting her reasoning.

"And what particular lesson did you hope to convey in the reading of this tale?"

"Hope."

"Hope?"

The other counselors were all still staring at her as though she was an apple in a barrel full of oranges. "You see, sometimes life can seem so bleak that we don't see all the good things around us. In addition, the story is a romantic, fun one."

Roarke couldn't believe what he was hearing. Sherry was making a mockery of the goals he'd set for this year's camp session. Romance! She wanted to teach her girls about some fickle female notion. The word alone was enough to make his blood run cold.

"Unfortunately, I disagree," Roarke said. "In the rational world there's no need for romantic nonsense." Although he tried to avoid looking at Sherry, his gaze refused to leave her. She looked flustered and embarrassed, and a fetching shade of pink had invaded her cheeks. Her gaze darted nervously to those around her, as if hoping to find someone who would agree with her. None would, Roarke could have told her that. His gaze fell to her lips, which were slightly moist and parted. Roarke's stomach muscles tightened and he hurriedly looked away. Love clouded the brain, he reminded himself sternly. The important things in life were found in education. Learning was the challenge. He should know. By age fifteen, he'd been a college student, graduating with full honors three years later. There'd been no time or need for trivial romance.

Sherry had seen Roarke's lips compress at the mention of romance, as though he associated the word with sucking lemons. "People need a little love in their lives," Sherry asserted boldly, although she was shaking on the inside.

"I see," he said, when it was obvious that he didn't.

The meeting continued then, and the staff was dismissed fifteen minutes later. Sherry was the first one to vacate her chair, popping up like hot bread out of a toaster the second the meeting was adjourned. She had to get back to the cabin to see if Ralph had been caught and peace had once again been restored to the seven wizards' cabin.

"Miss White." Roarke stopped her.

"Yes." Sherry's heart bounded to her throat. Damn, she'd hoped to make a clean getaway.

"Would it be possible for you to drop by my office later this afternoon?" The references—she knew it; he'd discovered they'd been falsified.

Their eyes met. Sherry's own befuddled brown clashed with Roarke's tawny-hazel. His open challenge stared down her hint of defiance, and Sherry dropped her gaze first. "This afternoon? S-sure," she answered finally, with false cheerfulness. At least he'd said afternoon rather than morning, so if Lynn was right she didn't need to start packing her bags yet. She released a grateful sigh and smiled. "I'll be there directly after lunch."

"Good."

He turned and Sherry charged from the meeting room and sprinted across the grounds with the skill of an Olympic runner. Oh heavens, she prayed Ralph had returned to his home. Life wouldn't be so cruel as to break Pamela's heart—would it?

Back at the cabin, Sherry discovered Pamela sitting on her bunk, crying softly.

"No Ralph?"

All seven children shook their heads simultaneously.

Sherry's heart constricted. "Please don't worry."

"I want Ralph," Pamela chanted, holding the pillow to her stomach and rocking back and forth. "Ralph's the only friend I ever had."

Sherry glanced around, hoping for a miracle. Where was Sherlock Holmes when she really needed him?

"He popped his head up between the floorboards a while ago," Sally explained, doubling over to peek underneath her bunk on the off chance he was there now.

"He's afraid of her microscope," Gretchen said accusingly. "I'm convinced that sweet hamster was worried sick that he'd end up in a jar like those . . . those pigs."

"He knows I wouldn't do that," Sally shouted, placing her hands defiantly on her hips, her eyes a scant inch from Gretchen's.

"Girls, please," Sherry pleaded. "We're due in the mess hall in five minutes."

A shriek arose as they scrambled for their clothes. Only Pamela remained on her bed, unmoved by the thought of being late for breakfast.

Sherry joined the little girl and folded her arm across the small shoulders. "We'll find him."

Tears glistened in the bright blue eyes. "Do you promise?"

Sherry didn't know what to say. She couldn't guarantee something like that. Pamela was a mathematical genius, so Sherry explained in terms the child would understand. "I can't make it a hundred per cent. Let's say seventy-five/twenty-five." For heaven's sake just how far could one hamster get? "Now, get dressed and go into the dining room with dry eyes."

Pamela nodded and climbed off her cot.

"Girls!" Sherry raised her hand to gain their attention. The loud chatter died to a low hum. "Remember, Ralph is our little secret!" The campers knew the rules better than Sherry. Each one was well aware that keeping Ralph was an infraction against camp policy.

"Our lips are sealed." Jan and Jill pantomimed zipping their mouths closed.

"After breakfast, when you've gone to your first class, I'll come back here and look for Ralph. In the meantime I think we'd best pretend nothing's unusual." Her questioning eyes met Pamela's, and Sherry gave her a reassuring hug.

With a gallant effort, Pamela sniffed and nodded. "I just want my Ralphie to come home."

After the frenzied search that had resulted from his disappearance, Sherry couldn't have agreed with the little girl more.

Before they left the cabin for the dining room, Sherry set the open shoe box in the middle of the cabin floor in the desperate hope that the runaway would find his own way home. She paused to close the door behind her charges and glanced over her shoulder with the fervent wish: *Ralph, please come home!*

In the dining hall, seated around the large circular table for eight, Sherry noted that none of her girls showed much of an appetite. French toast should have been a popular breakfast, but for all the interest her group showed, the cook could have served mush!

As the meal was wearing down, Mr. Roarke stepped forward.

"Isn't he handsome?" Gretchen said, looking toward Sherry. "My mother could really go for a man like him."

After what had happened that morning, Sherry was more than willing to let Gretchen's mother take Jeff Roarke. Good luck to her. With his views on romance she'd be lucky if she made it to first base.

"He does sort of look like a Prince Charming," Sally agreed.

"Mr. Roarke?" Sherry squinted, narrowing her gaze, wondering what kind of magic Roarke used on women.

Young and old seemed to find him overwhelmingly attractive.

"Oh, yes," Sally repeated with a dreamy look clouding her eyes. "He's just like the prince you read about in the story last night."

Sherry squinted her eyes again in an effort to convince the girls she couldn't possibly be interested in him as a romantic lead in her life.

Standing in front of the room, his voice loud and clear without a microphone, Roarke made the announcements for the day. The highlight of the first week of camp was a special guest speaker who would be giving a talk on the subject of fungus and mold. Roarke was sure the campers would all enjoy hearing Dr. Waldorf speak. From the eager nods around the room, Sherry knew he was right.

Fungus? Mold? Sally looked as excited as if he'd announced a tour of a candy factory that would be handing out free samples. Maybe Sherry was wrong. Maybe her charges weren't really children. Perhaps they really were dwarfs. Because if they were children, they certainly didn't act like any she'd ever known.

Following breakfast, all fifty wizards emptied the dining room and headed for their assigned classes. Sherry wasted little time in returning to her cottage.

The shoe box stood forlornly in the middle of the room. Empty. No Ralph.

Kneeling beside the box, Sherry took a piece of squished French toast from her jeans pocket and ripped it into tiny pieces, piling them around the shoe box. "Ralph," she called out softly. "You love Pamela, don't you? Surely you don't want to break the sweet little girl's heart."

An eerie sensation ran down her spine, as though someone were watching her. Slowly Sherry turned to find a large calico cat sitting on the ledge of the open window. His almond eyes narrowed into thin slits as he surveyed the room.

A cat!

"Shoo!" Sherry screamed, shooting to her feet. She whipped out her hands in an effort to chase the monster away. She didn't know where in the devil he'd come from, but he certainly wasn't welcome around here. Not with Ralph on the loose. When the cat ran off, and with her heart pounding, Sherry shut and latched the window.

By noon, she was tired of looking for Ralph—tired of trying to find a hole or a crack large enough to hide a hamster. An expedition into the deepest, darkest jungles of Africa would have been preferable to this. She joined the girls in the dining room and sadly shook her head when seven pairs of hope-filled eyes silently questioned her on the fate of the hamster. Pamela's bottom lip trembled and tears brimmed in her clear blue eyes, but she didn't say anything.

The luncheon menu didn't fare much better than breakfast. The girls barely ate. Sherry knew she'd made a terrible mistake in allowing Pamela to keep the hamster. She'd gone against camp policy and now was paying the price. Rules were rules. She should have known better.

After lunch, the girls once again went their separate ways. With a heavy heart, Sherry headed for Roarke's office. He answered her knock and motioned for her to sit down. Sherry moistened her dry lips as the girls' comment about Roarke being a prince came to mind. At the time, she'd staunchly denied any attraction she felt for him. To the girls and to herself. Now, alone with him in his office, Sherry's reaction to him was decidedly positive. If she were looking for someone to fill the role of Prince Charming in her life, only one man need apply. She found it amusing, even touching, that somehow even in glasses, this man was devastating. He apparently wore them for reading, but he hadn't allowed the staff to see him in them before now.

"Before I forget, how did you settle the problem with Gretchen Hamburg?"

"Ah yes, Gretchen." Proud of herself, Sherry leaned back in the chair and crossed her legs. "It was simple actually. I repositioned her cot away from the wall. That was all she really wanted."

"And she's satisfied with that?"

"Relatively. The mattress is too flat, the pillow's too soft and the blanket's too thin, but other than that, the bed is fine."

"You handled that well."

Sherry considered that high praise coming from her fearless director. He, too, leaned back in his chair. He hesitated and seemed to be considering his words as he rolled a pencil between his palms. "I feel that I may have misled you when you applied for the position at Camp Gitche Gumee," he said after a long pause.

"Oh?" Her heart was thundering at an alarming rate.

"We're not a Camp Fire Girl camp."

Sherry didn't breathe, fearing what was coming next. "I beg your pardon?"

"This isn't the usual summer camp."

Sherry couldn't argue with that—canoeing and hiking were offered, but there was little else in the way of fun camping experiences.

"Camp Gitche Gumee aspires to academic excellence," he explained, with a thoughtful frown. "We take the brightest young minds in this country and challenge them to excel in a wide variety of subjects. As you probably noted from the announcements made this morning, we strive toward bringing in top educators to lecture on stimulating subjects."

"Like *fungus and mold*?"

"Yes. Dr. Waldorf is a world-renowned lecturer. Fascinating subject." Roarke tried to ignore her sarcastic tone. From the way she was staring back at him, he realized she strongly disapproved, and he was surprised at how much her puckered frown affected him. Something deep inside him yearned to please her, to draw the light of her smile back into her eyes, to be bathed in the glow of her approval. The thought froze him. Something was drastically wrong with him. With restrained anger, he pushed his glasses up the bridge of his nose.

Her lack of appreciation for the goals he'd set for this summer put him in an uncomfortable position. She saw him as a stuffed shirt, that much was obvious, but he couldn't allow Sherry's feelings to cloud his better judgment. He didn't want to destroy her enthusiasm, but it was necessary to guide it into the proper channels. He liked Sherry's spirit, even though she'd made it obvious she didn't agree with his methods. He hesitated once more. He didn't often talk about his youth, saw no reason to do so, but it was important to him that Sherry understand.

"I would have loved a camp such as this when I was ten," he said thoughtfully.

"You?"

"It might astonish you to know that I was once considered a child prodigy."

It didn't surprise her, now that she thought about it.

"I was attending high-school classes when most boys my age were trying out for Little League. I was in college at fifteen and had my master's by the time I was twenty."

Sherry didn't know how to comment. The stark loneliness in his voice said it all. He'd probably had few friends and little or no contact with other children like himself. The pressures on him would have crumpled anyone else.

Jeff Roarke's empty childhood had led him to establish Camp Gitche Gumee. His own bleak experiences were what made the camp so important to him. A surge of compassion rose within Sherry and she gripped her hands together.

"Learning can be fun," she suggested softly, after a long moment. "What about an exploration into the forests in search of such exotic animals as the salamander and tree frog?"

"Yes, well, that is something to consider."

"And how about camp songs?"

"We sing."

"In Latin!"

"Languages are considered a worthy pursuit."

"Okay, games," Sherry challenged next. Her voice was raised as she warmed to her subject. She knew she wouldn't be able to hold her tongue long. It was better to get her feelings into the open than to try to bury them. "And I don't mean Camp Gitche Gumee's afternoon quiz teams, either."

"There are plenty of scheduled free times."

"But not organized fun ones," Sherry cried. "As you said, these children are some of the brightest in the country, but they have one major problem." She was all the way to the edge of her cushion by now, liberally using her hands for emphasis. "They have never been allowed to be children."

Once again, Roarke shoved his glasses up the bridge of his nose, strangely unsettled by her comments. She did make a strong case, but there simply wasn't enough time in a day to do all that she suggested. "Learning in and of itself should offer plenty of fun."

"But—"

Sherry wasn't allowed to finish.

"But you consider fairy tales of value?" he asked, recalling the reason he'd called her into his office.

"You're darn right I do. The girls loved them. Do you know Diane Miller? She's read Milton and Wilde and hasn't a clue who Dr. Seuss is."

"Who?" He blinked.

"Dr. Seuss." It wasn't until then that Sherry realized that Roarke knew nothing of Horton and the Grinch. He'd probably never tasted green eggs with ham or known about Sam.

Roarke struggled to disguise his ignorance. "I'm convinced your intentions are excellent, Miss White, but these parents have paid good money for their children to attend this camp with the express understanding that the children would learn. Unfortunately, fairy tales weren't listed as an elective on our brochure."

"Maybe they should have been," Sherry said firmly. "From everything I've seen, this camp is so academically minded that the entire purpose of sending a child away for the summer has been lost."

Roarke's mouth compressed and his eyes glinted coldly. Sherry could see she'd overstepped her bounds.

"After one week you consider yourself an expert on the subject?"

"I know children."

His hands shuffled the papers on his desk. "It was my understanding that you were a college senior."

"With a major in education."

"And a minor in partying?"

"That's not true," Sherry cried, coming to her feet.

Roarke rose as well, planted his hands on the desktop, and leaned forward. "Fairy tales are out, Miss White. In the evening you will prepare a study plan and have it approved by me. Is that understood?"

Sherry could feel the hot color fill her face. "Yes, sir," she responded crisply, and mocked him with a salute. If he was going to act like a marine sergeant then she'd respond like a lowly recruit.

"That was unnecessary!"

Sherry opened her mouth to argue with him when the calico cat she'd witnessed earlier in her cabin window suddenly appeared. A gasp rose in her throat at the tiny figure dangling from the cat's mouth.

"Ralph!" she cried, near hysteria.

Chapter Four

Ralph?" Roarke demanded. "Who the hell is Ralph?"

"Pamela's hamster. For heaven's sake do something!" Sherry cried. "He's still alive."

Slowly, Roarke advanced toward the cat. "Buttercup," he said softly. "Nice Buttercup. Put down..." He paused, twisting his head to look at Sherry.

"Ralph," Sherry supplied.

Roarke turned back to the cat. "I thought you said the name was Pamela."

"No, Ralph is Pamela's hamster."

"Right." He wiped a hand across his brow and momentarily closed his eyes. This just wasn't his day. Cautiously, he lowered himself to his knees.

Sherry followed suit, shaking with anxiety. Poor Ralph! Trapped in the jaws of death.

"Buttercup," Roarke encouraged softly. "Put down Ralph."

The absurdity of Roarke's naming a cat "Buttercup" unexpectedly struck Sherry, and a laugh oddly mingled with hysteria worked its way up her throat and escaped with the words, "The cat's name is Buttercup?"

This wasn't the time to explain that his mother had named the cat. "Buttercup isn't any more unusual than a hamster named Ralph!" Roarke said through gritted teeth.

Sherry snickered. "Wanna bet?"

Proud of her catch, Buttercup sat with the squirming rodent in her mouth, seeming to wait for the praise due her. Roarke, down on all fours, slowly advanced toward the feline.

"Will she eat him?" That was Sherry's worst fear. In her mind she could see herself as a helpless witness to the slaughter.

"I don't know what she'll do to him," Roarke whispered impatiently.

By now they were both down on all fours, in front of the sleek calico.

"I'll try to take him out of her mouth."

"What if she won't give him up?" Sherry was about an inch away from pressing the panic button.

Lifting his hand so slowly that it was difficult to tell that Roarke was moving, he gently patted the top of Buttercup's head.

"For heaven's sake don't praise her," Sherry hissed. "That's Pamela's hamster your cat is torturing."

"Here, Buttercup," he said soothingly, "give me Ralph."

The cat didn't so much as blink.

"I see she's well trained." Sherry couldn't resist the remark.

Roarke flashed her an irritated glance.

Just then the phone rang. Startled, Sherry bolted upright and her hand slapped her heart. A gasp died on her lips as Buttercup dropped Ralph and shot across the room. Roarke dived for the hamster, falling forward so that his elbow hit the floor with a solid thud. His glasses went flying.

"Got him," Roarke shouted triumphantly.

The phone pealed a second time.

"Here."

Without warning or option, Roarke handed Sherry the hamster. Her heart was hammering in her throat as the furry critter burrowed deep into her cupped hands. "Poor baby," she murmured, holding him against her chest.

"Camp Gitche Gumee," Roarke spoke crisply into the telephone receiver. "Just one moment and I'll transfer your call to the kitchen."

Sherry heard him punch a couple of buttons and hang up. In a sitting position on the floor, she released a long, ragged breath and slumped against the side of the desk, needing its support. At the rate her heart was pumping, she felt as if she had just completed the hundred-yard dash.

Roarke moved away from her and she saw him reach down and retrieve his glasses.

"How is he?" he asked, concerned.

"Other than being frightened half to death, he appears to be unscathed."

Silence.

"I . . . I suppose I should get Ralph back to the cabin," she said, feeling self-conscious and silly.

"Here, let me help you up." He gave her his hand, firmly clasping her elbow, and hauled her to her feet. Sherry found his touch secure and warm. And surprisingly pleasant. Very pleasant. As she stood she discovered that they were separated by only a few inches.

"Yes...well," she said and swallowed awkwardly. "Thank you for your help."

His eyes held hers. Lynn was right, Sherry noted. They weren't hazel but green, a deep cool shade of green that she associated with emeralds. Another surprise was how dark and expressive his eyes were. But the signals he was sending were strong and conflicting. Sherry read confusion and a touch of shock, as though she'd unexpectedly thrown him off balance.

Roarke's gaze dropped from her eyes to her mouth and Sherry's breath seemed to jam in her lungs.

She knew what Roarke wanted. The muscles of her stomach tightened and a sinking sensation attacked her with the knowledge that she would like it if he kissed her. The thought of his mouth fitting over hers was powerfully appealing. His lips would be like his hand, warm and firm. Sherry pulled herself up short. She was flabbergasted to be entertaining such thoughts. Jeff Roarke. Dictator! Marine sergeant! Stuffed shirt!

"Thank you for your help," she muttered in a voice hardly like her own. Hurriedly, she took a step in retreat, unable to escape fast enough.

Roarke stood stunned as Sherry backed away from him. He was shaking from the inside out. He'd nearly kissed her! And in the process gone against his own policy, and worse, his better judgment. Fortunately, whatever had been happening to him hadn't seemed to affect her. She'd jumped away from him as though she'd been burned, as if the thought of his kissing her was repulsive to her. Even then, it had taken all the strength of his will not to reach out and bring her into his arms.

Sherry watched as Roarke's mouth twisted into a mocking smile. "When you return to your cottage, Miss White, I suggest you read page 36 of the camp manual."

Without looking, Sherry already knew what it said: no pets! Well, anyone with half a brain in his head would recognize that Ralph wasn't a pet—he was a mascot. In her opinion every cabin should have one, but Sherry already knew what Roarke thought of her ideas.

"Miss White." He stopped her at the office door.

The softness in his accusing voice filled her with dread. "Yes?"

"I'd like to review your lesson plans for the evening sessions for the next week at your earliest convenience."

"I'll . . . I'll have them to you by tomorrow morning."

"Thank you."

"N-no," she stammered. "Thank you. I thought we'd lost Ralph for sure."

Sherry didn't remember walking across the campgrounds. The next thing she knew, she was inside the cabin and Ralph was safely tucked inside his shoe-box home.

Her heart continued to pound frantically and she sank onto the closest available bunk, grateful that Ralph had been found unscathed. And even more grateful that the issue of her application form and the references had been pushed to the side.

As much as she'd like to attribute her shaky knees and battering heart to Buttercup's merciless attack on Ralph, Sherry knew otherwise. It was Roarke. Like every other female in this camp, she had fallen under his magical spell. For one timeless moment she'd seen him as the others did. Attractive. Compelling. Dynamic. Jeff Roarke! There in his office, with Ralph in her hand, they'd gazed at each other and Sherry had been stunned into breathlessness. She wiped a hand over her eyes to shake the vivid image of the man from her mind. Her tongue moistened her lips as she imagined Roarke's mouth over hers. She felt herself melting inside and closed her eyes. It would have been good. Very, very good.

It took Sherry at least ten minutes to gather her composure, and she was grateful she'd kept her wits about her. It wasn't so unusual to be physically attracted to a man, she reassured herself. She had been plenty of times before; this wasn't really something new, and it was only an isolated incident. Wasn't it? As a mature adult, she was surely capable of keeping her hormones under control. For the remainder of the summer she would respond to Roarke with cool politeness, she decided. If he were to guess her feelings, she would be at his mercy.

Somehow, Sherry got through the rest of the day. Peace reigned in the cabin, and when the evening session came, Sherry read her young charges the story of Snow White and the Seven Dwarfs. She'd promised them she would, and she wouldn't go back on her word. But to be on the safe side, she also decided to teach them a song.

"Okay, everyone stand," she instructed, when she'd finished the story.

Simultaneously, seven pajama-clad preteens rose to their feet.

"What are we going to do now?" Gretchen cried. "I want to talk about Snow White."

"We'll discuss the story later." Sherry put off the youngster, and extended her hands. "Okay, everyone, this is a fun song, so listen up."

When she had their attention, she swayed her hips and pointed to her feet, singing at the top of her lungs how the anklebone was connected to the legbone and the legbone was connected to the hipbone. Seven small hips did an imitation of Sherry's gyrating action. Then the girls dissolved into helpless giggles. Soon the entire cabin was filled with the sounds of joy and laughter.

To satisfy her young charges, Sherry was forced into re-
peating the silly song no less than three times. At least if
she were asked to report tomorrow on their evening activity, Sherry would honestly be able to say that they'd studied the human skeleton. It felt good to have outsmarted
Roarke.

"Five minutes until lights-out," Sherry called, making
a show of checking her watch. From the corner of her eye,
she saw the girls scurry across the room and back to their
cots.

"I still want to talk about Snow White," Gretchen cried,
above the chaos. "You told me we'd have time to discuss
the story."

"I'm sorry," Sherry admitted contritely, sitting on the
edge of the young girl's mattress. "We really don't—not
tonight."

"But when the lights go out, that doesn't mean we have
to go to sleep."

"Yeah," another voice shouted out. Sherry thought it
came from Diane, the reader.

"Someone—anyone, turn out the lights," Sally cried.
"Then we can talk."

The room went dark.

Gretchen's bed was closest to the cabin entrance. The
room felt stuffy, so Sherry opened the door to allow in the
cool evening breeze. A soft ribbon of golden light from the
full moon followed the whispering wind inside the cabin.

"Did any of you know that Camp Gitche Gumee is
haunted?" Sherry whispered. The girls' attention was instant and rapt.

"There's no such thing as ghosts," Gretchen countered, but her tone lacked conviction.

"Oh, but there are." Sherry whispered, her own voice dipping to an eerie low. "The one who roams around here is named Longfellow."

"Oh, I get it," Diane said with a short laugh. "He was the author of the poem—"

"Shh." Sherry placed her index finger over her lips. Dramatically, she cupped her hands over her ears. "I think I hear him now."

The cabin went still.

"I hear something," Wendy whispered. In the moonlight, Sherry could see the ten-year-old had all ten of her Barbies and Kens in bed with her.

"You needn't worry." Sherry was quick to assure the girls. "Longfellow is a friendly ghost. He only does fun, good things."

"What kind of things?"

"Hmm, let me think."

"I bet Longfellow brought Ralph back."

Sherry hadn't told Pamela how Buttercup had captured the hamster. Her pet's narrow escape from the jaws of death would only terrorize the softhearted little girl.

"Now that I think about it, Pamela, you're right. Longfellow must have had a hand in finding Ralph."

"What other kinds of things does Longfellow do?" Jan and Jill wanted to know. As always, they spoke in unison. Jill's front tooth was still intact, but it wouldn't last much longer with the furious way she worked at extracting it.

"He finds missing items like socks and hair clips. And sometimes, late at night when it's stone quiet, if you listen real, real hard, you can hear him sing."

"You can?"

"Actually, he whistles," Sherry improvised.

The still room went even quieter as seven pairs of ears strained to listen to the wind whisper through the forest of redwoods outside their door.

"I hear him," Diane said excitedly. "He's real close."

"When I was a little kid," Sally told the group excitedly, "I used to be afraid of ghosts, but Longfellow sounds like a good ghost."

"Oh, he is."

"Can you tell us another story?" Gretchen pleaded. "They're fun."

For the chronic grumbler to ask for a fairy tale and admit anything was fun was almost more than Sherry could comprehend. "I think one more story wouldn't hurt," she said. "But that has to be all." Remembering the conversation with Roarke earlier that afternoon, Sherry felt a fleeting sadness. After tonight, her stories would have to come from more acceptable classics. She thought her girls were missing a wonderful part of their heritage as children by skipping fairy tales. If she didn't want this job so badly, Sherry would have battled Roarke more strenuously.

Leaning back against the wall, she brought her knees up to her chin, sighed audibly while she chose the tale, and started. "Once upon a time in a land far, far away..."

By the time she announced that "they lived happily ever after" the cabin was filled with the even, measured breathing of sleeping children. If the girls weren't all asleep they were close to it.

Gretchen snored softly, and taking care not to wake the slumbering child, Sherry climbed off her cot and checked on the others. She pulled a blanket around Jan's and Jill's shoulders and removed inanimate objects from the cots, placing Sally's microscope on the headboard and rescuing the Barbies and Kens from being crushed during the night.

Ralph was firmly secured in his weathered home, and Sherry gently slid the shoe box from underneath Pamela's arm.

"Sleep tight," she whispered to the much-loved rodent. "Or else I'll call Buttercup back."

As she moved to close the cabin door, Sherry was struck by how peaceful the evening was. Drawn outside, she sat on the top step of the large front porch and gazed at the stars. They were out in brilliant display this evening, scattered diamonds tossed on thick folds of black velvet. How close they seemed. Sparkling. Radiant.

Sherry's hands cupped her chin as she rested her elbows on her knees and studied the heavens.

"Good evening, Miss White." Roarke had heard their singing earlier, had come to investigate and had been amused by her efforts to outwit him.

The sound of Roarke's voice broke into Sherry's thoughts. "Good evening, Mr. Roarke," she responded crisply, and straightened. "What brings you out tonight?" Lordy, she hoped he hadn't been around to hear the last fairy tale, or worse, her mention of Longfellow.

He paused, braced one foot against the bottom step and looked over the grounds. "I like to give the camp a final check before turning in for the night."

"Oh." For the life of her, she couldn't think of a single thing more to say. Her reaction to him was immediate. Her heart pounded like a jackhammer and the blood shot through her veins. She'd like to fool herself into believing the cause was the unexpectedness of his arrival, but she knew better.

"How's Ralph?" Roarke questioned.

"Fully recovered. How's Buttercup?"

"Exceptionally proud." The soft laugh that followed was so pleasant sounding that it caused Sherry to smile just listening to him.

"You have a nice laugh." She hadn't meant to tell him that, but it slipped out before she could stop herself. As often was the case when she spoke to Jeff Roarke, the filter between her brain and her mouth malfunctioned and whatever she was thinking slid out without forethought.

"I was about to tell you how effervescent *your* laugh sounds."

Sherry couldn't remember a time she'd ever given him the opportunity to hear her laugh. The circumstances in which they were together prohibited it. Staff meetings were intensely serious. No one dared show any amusement.

"When—"

"Tonight. I suppose you plan to tell me that the leg-bone connected to the hipbone is a study of the human skeleton?"

Words ran together and tripped over the tip of her tongue. "Of course not . . . well, yes, but . . ."

He laughed again. "The girls thoroughly enjoyed it, didn't they?"

"Yes."

"That sort of education wasn't exactly what I had in mind, but anything is better than those blasted fairy tales."

Sherry was forced into sitting on her hands to keep from elbowing him. Fairy tales weren't silly or senseless. They served a purpose! But she managed to keep her thoughts to herself—with some effort.

Silence again.

"I have my lesson plan if you'd like to see it," she said, and started to get up, but his hand on her forearm stopped her.

"Tomorrow morning is soon enough."

He surprised her even more by climbing the three steps and taking a seat beside her. He paused and raised his eyes to the sky.

"Lovely, isn't it?" he asked.

"Yes." The one word seemed to strangle in her throat. Roarke was close enough to touch. All Sherry would have had to do was shift her weight for her shoulder to gently graze his. Less than an inch separated their thighs. Although she strove to keep from experiencing the physical impact of brushing against him, there was little she could do about the soft scent of the after-shave Roarke wore, which was so masculinely appealing. Every breath she drew in was more tantalizing than the one before. Spice and man—a lethal combination.

It was the night, Sherry decided, not the man. Oh, please, not the man, she begged. She didn't want to be so strongly attracted to Jeff Roarke. She didn't want to be like all the others. The two of them were so different. They couldn't agree on anything. Not him. Not her.

Neither spoke, but the silence wasn't a serene one. The darkness seemed charged with static electricity. Twice Sherry opened her mouth, ready to start some banal conversation simply to break the silence. Both times she found herself incapable of speaking. When she chanced a look in his direction she discovered his thick eyebrows arched bewilderedly over a storm cloud of sea-green eyes.

Naturally, neither one of them had the courage to introduce the phenomenon occurring between them into casual conversation. But Sherry was convinced Roarke felt the tug of physical attraction as strongly and powerfully as she did. And from the look of him, he was as baffled as she.

"Well, I suppose I should turn in," she said, after the longest minute of her life.

"I suppose I should, too."

But neither of them moved.

"It really is a lovely night," Sherry said, looking to the heavens, struck once again by the simple beauty of the starlit sky.

"Yes, lovely," Roarke repeated softly, but he wasn't gazing at the heavens, he was looking at Sherry. He'd believed everything he'd said to her about romance being nonsense, but now the words came back to haunt him. Right now, this moment with her seemed more important than life itself. He felt trapped in a whirlpool of awareness. The sensations that churned inside him were lethal to his mental health and he wouldn't alter a one. This woman had completely thrown him off balance with the unexpected flaring need he felt to hold her in his arms. Slipping his arm around her shoulder seemed the most natural act in the world...and strictly against his own camp policy. The urge to do so was so strong that he crossed his arms across his chest in an effort to keep them still. He was stunned at how close he'd come to giving in to temptation. Stunned and appalled.

Whatever caused Sherry to turn to meet his gaze, she didn't know. Fate, possibly. But she did rotate her head so that her eyes were caught by his as effectively as if trapped in a vise. Mesmerized, their gazes locked in the faint light of the glorious moon. It was as though Sherry were looking at him for the first time—through a love-struck teen's adoring eyes. He was devastatingly handsome. Dark, and compellingly masculine.

Unable to stop herself, she raised her hand, prepared to outline his thick eyebrows with her fingertips, and paused halfway to his face. His troubled eyes were a mirror of her own doubtful expression, Sherry realized. Yet his were charged with curiosity. He seemed to want to hold her in his arms as much as she yearned to let him. His mouth appeared to hunger for the taste of hers just as she longed to sample his. His shallow breath mingled with her labored one. Deep grooves formed at the sides of his mouth, and when his lips parted, Sherry noted that his breathing was hesitant.

Driven by something stronger than her own common sense, Sherry slowly, inch by inch, lowered her lashes, silently bending to his unspoken demand. Her own lips parted in welcome as her pulse fluttered wildly at the base of her throat.

Roarke lowered his mouth to a scant inch above hers.

Sherry was never sure what happened. A sound perhaps. A tree branch scraping against the roof of the cabin—perhaps an owl's screeching cry as it flew overhead. Whatever it was instantly brought her to her senses, and she was eternally grateful. She jerked her head back and willfully checked her watch.

"My goodness," she cried in a wobbly, weak voice, "will you look at the time?"

"Time?" he rasped.

"It's nearly eleven. I really must get inside." Already she was on her feet, rushing toward the front door as though being chased by a mad dog.

Not waiting for a response from Roarke, Sherry closed the door and weakly leaned against it. Her heart was thumping like a locomotive gone out of control. Her mouth felt dry and scratchy. Filled with purpose, she walked over to the small sink and turned on the cold water faucet. She gulped down the first glass in huge swallows and automatically poured herself a second. In different circumstances, she would have taken her temperature. There was something in the air. Sherry almost wished it was a virus.

*　*　*

The next morning, Sherry was on time for the staff meeting. She hadn't slept well and was awake even before the alarm sounded. At least when she was a few minutes early she could choose her own seat. The back of the room all but invited her and she claimed a seat there.

Lynn Duffy scooted in beside her.

"Morning," Sherry greeted her.

"Hi. How's it going?"

Sherry pushed the cuticle back on her longest fingernail. "Just fine. The kids are great."

"You got Gretchen Hamburg—don't tell me everything's fine. I know better."

"She's a cute kid!"

"Gretchen?" Lynn grumbled. "You've got to be teasing. The kid's a royal pain in the rear end!"

Two days ago, Sherry would have agreed with her, but from the minute Gretchen had announced that fairy tales were "fun" she'd won Sherry's heart.

Roarke stepped to the podium, and the small gathering of staff went silent. Sherry noted that he took pains not to glance in her direction, which was fine by her. She preferred that he didn't. This morning the memory of those few stolen moments alone under the stars was nothing short of embarrassing. She'd rather forget the entire episode. Chalk it up to the decreased layer of ozone in outer space. Or the way the planets were aligned. The moon was in its seventh house. Aquarius and Mars. A fluke certainly. She could look at him this morning and feel nothing . . . well, that wasn't exactly true. The irritation was gone, replaced by a lingering fascination.

After only a minimum of announcements, the staff were dismissed. Sherry stood, eager to make her escape.

"Sherry," Lynn said, following her out of the meeting room, "do you have some free time later?"

"After breakfast."

Her friend looked a bit chagrined. "I have to run into town. Would you like to come along?"

"Sure, I'll come over to your cabin after I get my wizards off to their first class."

Lynn brightened. "I'll look for you around eight, then."

Her friend took off in the opposite direction and Sherry's gaze followed the younger girl. Now that she thought about it, Lynn didn't seem to be her normal, cheerful self. Sherry had the impression that this jaunt into town was an excuse to talk.

It was.

The minute Sherry got into Lynn's car she could feel the other girl's coiled tension. Sherry was uncertain. She didn't know if she should wait until Lynn mentioned what was troubling her, or if she should say something to start Lynn talking. She chose the latter.

"Are you enjoying the camp this summer?" Sherry asked.

Lynn shrugged. "It's different."

"How's that?"

Again her shoulders went up and down in a dismissive gesture. The long country road that led to the small city of Arrow Flats twisted and turned as it came down off the rugged hillside.

"Have you noticed Peter Towne?" Lynn said quietly.

"The lifeguard?"

"Yeah...it's his second year here, too. Last summer we were good friends. We even managed a few letters since then, Christmas, Easter and the like."

As Sherry recalled Peter was a handsome sun-bleached blonde who patrolled the beaches during the afternoons and worked in the kitchen after dinner. "How old is he?"

"Nineteen—the same age as me."

Whatever was troubling Lynn obviously had to do with Peter. "He seems to be nice enough," Sherry prodded.

"Peter is more than nice," Lynn said dreamily. "He's wonderful."

Sherry wouldn't have gone quite that far to describe him. "So you two worked together last year?"

"Right."

The teenager focused her attention on the roadway, which was just as well since it looked treacherous enough to Sherry.

"What makes you bring up his name?" Sherry ventured.

"Peter's?"

"Yes, Peter's."

"Did I bring him up?"

"Lynn, honestly, you know you did."

The other girl bit the corner of her bottom lip. "Yeah, I suppose his name did casually pop into the conversation."

It seemed to Sherry that Lynn regretted having said anything so she let the matter drop. "I had my first run-in with ol' Ironjaw."

"You mean Mr. Roarke?"

"He and I had a difference of opinion about the evening sessions. He'd prefer for me to discuss the intricacies of U.S. foreign policy. I'd rather tell ghost stories. I imagine we'll agree on a subject somewhere in between."

"I saw you put something on the podium for him this morning."

"Lesson plans."

"He's making you do that?"

"As a precaution."

"Oh."

Lynn eased the car to a stop at the crossroads before turning onto the main thoroughfare. Arrow Flats was about ten miles north of the camp. Sherry noticed the way Lynn's hands tightened around the steering wheel at the intersection.

"Two nights ago, I couldn't sleep," she said in a strained, soft voice. "I decided to take a walk down to the lake. There was an old piece of driftwood there so I sat down. Peter...couldn't sleep, either. He happened to come by, and we sat and talked."

"From everything I've seen, Peter's got a good head on his shoulders."

"It was nearly one before we went back to camp. He kissed me, Sherry. I never wanted anyone to kiss me more than Peter that night in the moonlight. It was so romantic and...I don't know...I've never felt this strongly about any boy before."

Sherry could identify with that from her own surprising experience with Roarke, the night before on the porch. Maybe there really was something in the air, she thought hopefully.

"Now every time I look at Peter I see the same longing in his eyes. We want to be together. I...I think we may be falling in love."

Sherry thought it was wonderful that the friendship between the two had blossomed into something more, but she understood her friend's dilemma. The camp was no place for a romance.

"Oh, Sherry, what am I going to do?" Lynn cried. "If Mr. Roarke finds out, both Peter and I will be fired."

Chapter Five

Good morning, Miss White."

Roarke's voice rose to greet her when Sherry slipped into the back row of chairs in the staff room. She muttered something appropriate, embarrassed once again to be caught coming in tardy for yet another early-morning session. On this particular day, her only excuse was laziness. The alarm had gone off and she simply hadn't been able to force herself out of bed.

As always, Roarke waited until she'd settled in her seat before continuing.

Sherry tried her best to listen to the day's announcements, but her mind drifted to Lynn and Peter and their predicament. It felt peculiar to side with Roarke, but Sherry agreed that a romance at camp could be a source of problems for the teenagers and everyone else. Lynn's attraction to Peter was a natural response for a nineteen-year-old girl, and Peter was a fine boy, but camp simply wasn't the place for their courtship. Sherry had advised her

friend to "cool it" as much as possible. In a couple of
months, once camp had been dismissed, the two could
freely date each other.

Sherry's gaze skidded from the tall blond youth back to
Lynn. They were doing their best to hide their growing affection for each other, but from the not-so-secret glances
they shared, their feelings were all too obvious to Sherry.
And if she could see how they felt, then it probably
wouldn't be long before Roarke did, too.

A chill ran up Sherry's arms, and she bundled her
sweater more tightly around her. She yawned and rubbed
the sleep from her eyes, forcing herself to pay attention to
what Roarke was saying.

The others were beginning to stand and move about before she realized that the session had come to a close. Still
she didn't move. Standing, walking about, thinking,
seemed almost more than she could manage. What she
needed was some kind soul to intravenously feed her coffee a half hour before the alarm went off.

"Is there a problem, Miss White?"

Sherry glanced up to find Roarke looming above her.

"No," she mumbled and shook her head for emphasis.

"Then shouldn't you be getting back to your cabin?"

She nodded, although that, too, required some effort.
A giant yawn escaped, and she cupped her hand over her
mouth. "I suppose."

"You really aren't a morning person, are you?"

Her smile was weak. "It just takes a while for my heart
to start working."

Roarke straddled a seat in the row in front of her and
looped his arm over the chair back as he studied her. She
looked as though she could curl up right there and without much effort go back to sleep. The urge to wrap her in
his arms and press her head against his shoulder was a

powerful one. He could almost feel her softness yield against his muscled strength. Forcibly, he shook the image from his mind. His gaze softened as he studied her. "Did you hear anything of what I said?"

"A... little," she admitted sheepishly. He grinned at that, and she discovered that his smile completely disarmed her. Speaking of getting her heart revved up! One smile from Jeff Roarke worked wonders. No man had the right to look that good this early in the day. Her mind had come up with a list of concrete arguments for him to postpone these sessions to a more decent time of day, but one charming look shot them down like darts tossed at fat balloons. "I don't know what it is about mornings, but I think I may be allergic to them."

"Perhaps if you tried going to bed earlier."

"It doesn't work," she said, and yawned again. "I wish I could, but at about ten every night, I come alive. My best work is done then."

Roarke glanced at his watch, nodded and stood. "Your cabin is due in the mess hall in fifteen minutes."

Sherry groaned and dropped her feet. Her hand crisply touched her forehead. "Aye, aye, Commandant, we'll be there."

Roarke chuckled and returned her mock salute.

When Sherry entered the cabin, she discovered the girls in a frenzy. Pamela had climbed to the top of the dresser and was huddled into a tight ball clutching Ralph, her knees drawn up against her chest. Gretchen faced the open door, a broom raised above her head, prepared for attack, while Jan and Jill were nearby, holding their shoes in their fists like lethal weapons.

Ginny, the high-school girl who had been assigned to stay in the cabin while Sherry was at the morning meeting, was in as much of a tizzy as the girls.

"What happened?" Sherry demanded.

"He tried to kill Ralph," Pamela screamed hysterically.

"Who?"

"I read about things like this," Diane inserted calmly. "It's a natural instinct."

"What is?" Sherry cried, hurriedly glancing from girl to girl.

"The cat," Jan and Jill said together.

"Ralph was nearly eaten," Pamela cried.

Sherry sagged with relief. "That's only Buttercup."

"Buttercup!"

"He belongs to Mr. Roarke."

"Mr. Roarke has a cat named Buttercup?" Gretchen said, lowering her broom to the floor. A look of astonishment relaxed her mouth into a giant O.

"Apparently so."

"But he tried to get Ralph." Pamela opened her hands and the rodent squirmed his head out between two fingers and looked around anxiously.

"We need a cage," Sherry said decisively. "That shoe box is an open invitation to Buttercup."

"Can't Mr. Roarke keep his cat chained up or something?" Wendy suggested. The Barbies and Kens were scattered freely across the top of her mattress.

"I thought we weren't supposed to have pets," Gretchen complained. "I find Mr. Roarke's actions highly contradictory."

"Since we're keeping Ralph, mentioning Buttercup to Mr. Roarke wouldn't be wise," Sherry informed them all with a tight upper lip.

"But we've got to do something."

"Agreed." One glance at her watch confirmed that her troop was already late for breakfast. "Hurry now, girls. I'll take care of everything."

"Everything?" Pam's bold eyes studied her counselor.

"Everything," Sherry promised.

By the time Sherry and her cabin arrived at the mess hall, the meal was already half over. The stacks of pancakes had cooled and the butter wouldn't melt on them properly. Gretchen complained loudly enough for the cooks in the kitchen to hear.

In the middle of breakfast, Sally produced a huge tannish-gold hawk moth she'd trapped the night before and passed it around the table for the others to admire, momentarily distracting Sherry.

"Girls, manners. Please," she cried, when Wendy stuffed a whole pancake into her mouth. Sticky syrup oozed down the preteen's chin.

"But we have to hurry," Diane complained.

"You'll talk to Mr. Roarke about his cat, won't you?" Pam wanted to know as she climbed out of her chair, her meal untouched.

"I'll see what I can do."

When the last girl had left the dining room, rushing to her class, Sherry sighed with relief. She hadn't so much as had her first cup of coffee and already the morning was a disaster.

"Problems, Miss White?" Again Roarke joined her. He handed her a steaming mug of coffee.

She cupped it in her hands and savored the first sip. "Bless you."

Roarke pulled out a chair and sat down across the table from her.

"Buttercup paid us another visit," she said after a long moment.

"Ralph?"

"Is fine...."

His jaw tightened. "May I remind you, Miss White, that it is against camp policy to have a pet?"

"Ralph is a mascot, not a pet."

"He's a damn nuisance."

"You're a fine one to talk," she returned heatedly and took another sip of coffee in an effort to fortify her courage. "As for camp policy—what do you call Buttercup?"

"The camp cat."

"She's not a pet?"

"Definitely not."

"My foot!"

"If there are problems with Ralph, then the solution is simple—get rid of him."

"No way! Pamela's strongly attached to that animal." Surely Roarke wasn't heartless enough to take away a child's only friend. "This is the first time Pamela's spent more than a few days away from home and family. That hamster's helping her through the long separation from her brother and parents."

"If I allow Ralph to stay, then next year someone is likely to bring a boa constrictor and claim it's not a pet, either."

Sherry twisted her head from side to side, glancing around her. Lowering her voice, she leaned forward and whispered, "No one knows about Ralph. I'm not telling, the girls aren't telling. That only leaves you."

"Buttercup knows."

"She's the problem," Sherry gritted between clenched teeth.

"No," Roarke countered heatedly. "Ralph is."

From the hard set of the director's mouth, Sherry could see that discussing this matter would solve nothing. She held up both palms in a gesture of defeat. "Fine."

"Fine what? You'll get rid of Ralph?"

"No! I'll take care of the problem."

"How?" He eyed her dubiously.

"I haven't figured that out yet, but I will."

"That I don't doubt. Just make sure I don't know a thing about it."

"Right." Playfully, she winked at him, stood, reached for a small pancake, popped it into her mouth and left the dining hall. She understood Roarke's concerns, but occasional exceptions to rules had to be made. Life was filled with too many variables for him to be so hard-nosed and stringent. Ralph had to be kept a secret, and more than that, the rodent couldn't continue to rule the lives of her seven charges. A cage was one solution, but knowing Buttercup, that wouldn't be enough to distract the cat from her daily raids.

She found the answer in town. That night after the evening meal, Sherry carried in the solution for the girls to examine.

"What's it for?" Sally wanted to know when Sherry held the weapon up for their inspection.

Bracing her feet like a trained commando, Sherry looped the strap over her shoulder and positioned the machine gun between her side and her elbow. "One shot from this and Buttercup won't be troubling Ralph again."

"You aren't going to..." Jan began.

"...shoot him?" Jill finished her twin's worried query.

The girls' eyes widened as Sherry's mouth twisted into a dark scowl. "You bet. I'm going to shoot him—right between the eyes."

A startled gasp rose.

"Miss White," Pamela pleaded, "I don't want you to hurt Buttercup."

Sherry relaxed and lowered the machine gun, grinning. "Oh, I wouldn't do that. This is a battery-operated water gun."

"Really?"

"A water gun?" Diane asked, lowering her book long enough to examine Sherry's weapon.

"I knew that all along," Gretchen said.

"I'll show you how it works." Sherry aimed it at her bedroom door and fingered the trigger. Instantly, a piercing blast of water slammed against the pine door ten feet away.

"Hey, not bad," Diane said excitedly.

"It's as accurate as a real gun," Sherry explained further. "After a shot or two from this beauty, Buttercup won't come within fifty feet of this cabin."

The spontaneous applause gladdened Sherry's heart. She accepted the praise of her charges with a deep bow and placed the weapon in her bedroom. Returning a moment later, she entered the room with a dark visor pulled down low over her eyes. She held out a deck of cards toward them.

"Okay, girls, gather 'round," she called. "Tonight's lesson is about statistics." Grinning, she playfully shuffled the cards from one hand to the other. "Anyone here ever played gin rummy?"

If Sherry had thought her charges enjoyed the fairy tales, they were even more ecstatic about cards. Their ability to pick up the rules and the theory behind the games astonished her. It shouldn't, she mused. After all they were real live wizards! After she'd taught them the finer point of gin rummy, the seven had eagerly learned hearts and canasta. At nine-thirty, their scheduled bedtime, the girls didn't want to quit. Cards were fun, and there was precious little time for that commodity at Camp Gitche Gumee.

When the lights were out, Sherry lay in her own bed, wishing she could convince Jeff Roarke that camp, no matter what its specialty, was meant to be fun.

No longer did Sherry think of Roarke in negative terms. They still disagreed on most subjects, but the wall of annoyance and frustration she'd felt toward him had been a means of hiding the sensual awareness she experienced the minute he walked into the room. It pricked her pride to admit that she was like every other female over the age of ten at Camp Gitche Gumee. Jeff Roarke was as sexy as the day was long. And since this was June, the days were lengthy enough to weave into the nights.

Sherry expelled her breath and sat upright in the darkened room. It wasn't only thoughts of Roarke that were keeping her awake. Guilt played a hand in her troubled musings. Her father and Phyliss were probably worried sick about her. Leaving the way she had hadn't been one of her most brilliant schemes. By this time, no doubt, her stepmother had hired a detective agency to track her down.

Contrite feelings about her evening sessions with the girls also played a role in her sleeplessness. She'd handed in the lesson plans to Roarke knowing that she'd misled him a little. It was stretching even her vivid imagination to link canasta and gin rummy with statistics.

This summer had been meant to be carefree and fun, and Sherry was discovering that it was neither. Tossing aside the blankets, she reached for her jeans. The pay phone was situated on the campgrounds, directly across from her cabin. If she talked to her father, she'd feel better. There wasn't any need to let Phyliss know where she was, but it couldn't hurt to keep in touch.

Pulling her sweatshirt over her head, Sherry tiptoed between the bunks and quietly slipped out the front door. The night was filled with stars. A light breeze hummed across the treetops, their melody singing in the wind. Cotton-puff clouds roamed across the full moon, and the sweet scent of virgin forest filled the air. Tucking the tips of her fingers in her hip pockets, Sherry paused to examine the beauty of the world around her. It was lovely enough to take her breath away.

The pay phone was well lit, and Sherry slipped her quarters into the appropriate slot. Her father's groggy voice greeted her on the fourth ring.

"Hello?"

"Hi, Dad."

"Sherry?"

"How many other girls call you Dad?"

Virgil White chuckled. "You give me as much trouble as ten daughters."

"Honestly, Dad!"

"Sherry, where—"

Her father's voice was interrupted by a frenzied, eager one. "Oh, thank God," a female voice came over the line. "Sherry, darling, is that you?"

"Hello, Phyliss. Listen, I'm in a pay phone and I've only got a few quarters—"

"Virgil, do something.... Sherry's nearly penniless."

"Phyliss, I've got money, it's just quarters I'm short of at the moment. Please listen, I wanted you to know I'm fine."

"Are you eating properly?"

"Three meals a day," Sherry assured her.

"Liver once a week? Fresh fruit and vegetables?"

"Every day, scout's honor."

The sound of her father's muffled laugh came over the wire. "You were never a Girl Scout."

Phyliss gasped and started to weep silently.

"Dad, now look what you've done. Phyliss, I'm eating better than ever, and I have all the clothes I could possibly need."

"Money?"

"I'm doing just great. Wonderful, in fact. I don't need anything."

"Are you happy, baby?"

"Very happy," Sherry assured them both.

"Where are you—at least tell me where you are," her stepmother cried.

Before she could answer, the operator came back on the line. "It will be another $1.25 for the next three minutes."

"I've got to go."

"Sherry," Phyliss pleaded. "Remember to eat your garlic."

"I'll remember," she promised. "Goodbye, Dad. Goodbye, Phyliss." At age twenty-one she didn't require a baby-sitter, although Phyliss seemed convinced otherwise. As the good daughter, Sherry had done her duty.

Gently she replaced the telephone receiver, feeling much relieved. Looking up she discovered Roarke advancing toward her across the lawn in long, angry strides. Just the way he moved alerted her to his mood. She stiffened with apprehension and waited.

"Miss White." His gaze traveled from the telephone to her and then back again. "Who's staying with the girls?"

"I . . . they're all asleep. I didn't think it would matter if I slipped out for a couple of minutes. I'd be able to hear them if there was a problem," she went on hurriedly, trying to cover her guilty conscience. She really hadn't been gone more than a few minutes.

The anger left Roarke as quickly as it came. He knew he was being unreasonable. The source of his irritation wasn't that Sherry had stepped outside her cabin. It was the fact that she'd made a phone call, and he strongly suspected she'd contacted a male friend.

Self-consciously, Sherry lowered her head. "You're right, I shouldn't have left the girls. I'll make sure it doesn't happen again."

"It's a pleasure to have you agree to something I say," Roarke said, his face relaxing into a lazy smile.

Sherry's heart lifted in a strange, weightless way. She'd been tense, conscious once more that she'd done something to irritate him.

"I'll walk you back to your cabin," he suggested softly.

"Thank you." It wasn't necessary, for the cabin was within sight, but she was pleased Roarke chose to keep her company.

"I saw you on the phone," he commented, without emotion, a few minutes later. "I suppose you were talking to one of your boyfriends."

"No," she corrected, "that was my family."

Roarke cleared his throat and straightened. "Is there a boyfriend waiting for you back . . . where was it again?"

"Seattle, and no, not anyone I'm serious about." Sherry went still, her heart thundering against her breast. "And you? Do y-you have someone waiting in Berkeley?"

Roarke shook his head. There was Fiona, another professor whom he saw socially. They'd seen each other in a friendly sort of way for a couple of years, but he hadn't experienced any of the physical response with Fiona that he did with Sherry. Come to think of it, Fiona's views on romance were much like his own. "There's no one special," he said after a moment.

"I see." From the length of time that it took him to tell her that, Sherry suspected that there was someone. Her spirits dipped a little. Good grief, did she think he lived like a hermit? He couldn't! He was too damn good-looking.

Roarke's gaze studied her then, and in the veiled shadows of the moon, Sherry noted that it was impossible to make out the exact color of his eyes. Green or tawny, it didn't seem to matter now that they were focused directly on her. Her breathing became shallow and she couldn't draw her gaze away from him. Finally, she dragged her eyes from his and looked up at the stars.

Neither spoke for several minutes, and Sherry found the quiet disarming.

"You seem to have adjusted well to the camp," Roarke commented. "Other than a few problems with mornings, that is."

"Thank you."

"How did the lessons go this evening? Wasn't it statistics you told me you were planning to discuss?"

Sherry swallowed down her apprehension and answered in a small, quiet voice. "Everything went well."

Roarke's eyes narrowed as he watched her struggle to keep the color from invading her cheeks. She might think herself clever, but he wasn't completely ignorant of her creative efforts.

"I may have deviated a little," she admitted finally.

"A little?" Roarke taunted. "Then let me ask you something."

"Sure." She tried to make her voice light and airy, belying her nervousness.

"Who got stuck with the queen of spades?"

"Gretchen," she returned automatically, then slapped her hand over her mouth. "You know?"

"I had a fair idea. A little friendly game of hearts, I take it?"

She nodded, studying him. "And canasta and gin rummy, while I was at it."

He did nothing more than shake his head in a gesture of defeat.

"Are you going to lecture me?"

"Will it do any good?"

Sherry laughed softly. "Probably not."

"That's what I thought."

She relaxed, liking him more by the minute. "Then you don't mind?"

Roarke sighed. "As long as you don't fill their minds with romantic tales, I can live with it. But I'd like to ask about the lesson plans you handed in to me."

"Oh, I was planning to do everything I wrote down... I'm just using kind of... unorthodox methods."

"I figured as much." His face relaxed into a languorous smile. "I'd guess that the night you intend a study on finances is really a game of Monopoly."

"Yes... how'd you know?" He didn't sound irritated, and that lent Sherry confidence.

"I have my ways."

"Do you know everything that goes on in this camp?" She'd never met anyone like him. Roarke seemed to be aware of every facet of his organization. How he managed to keep tabs on each area, each cabin, was beyond her.

"I don't know everything," he countered, "but I try...."

As his voice trailed off the beauty of the night demanded their attention. Neither spoke for a long moment, but neither was inclined to leave, either.

"I find it surprising that you don't have someone special waiting for you." Roarke's voice was low, slightly bewildered.

"It's not so amazing." A few men had been attracted to her—before Phyliss had drilled them on their intentions, invited them to dinner and driven them crazy with her wackiness. A smile touched the corner of Sherry's mouth. If there was anyone she wished to discourage, all she need do was introduce him to her loony stepmother. "I'm attending Seattle Pacific full-time, and I'm involved in volunteer work. There isn't much opportunity to date."

While she was speaking, Roarke couldn't stop looking at her. Her profile was cast against the moon shadows of the dark violet sky. The light breeze flirted with her hair, picking up the wispy strands at her temple and puffing them out and away from her face. Her dark hair was thick and inviting. He thought about lifting it in his hands, running the silky length through his fingers, burying his face in it and breathing in its fresh, clean scent. From the moment she'd first entered his office he'd thought she was pretty. Now, Roarke studied her and saw much more than the outward loveliness that had first appealed to him. Her spirit was what attracted him, her love of life, her enthusiasm.

He'd never seen a cabin enjoy their counselor more. Sherry was a natural with the children. Inventive. Clever. Fun. A hundred times since she'd arrived at camp, he'd been angered enough to question the wisdom of having hired her. But not tonight, not when he was standing in the moonlight with her at his side. Not now, when he would have given a month's wages to taste her lips and feel her softness pressed against him. She was a counselor and he was the camp director, but tonight that would be so easy to forget. He was a man so strongly attracted to a woman that his heart beat with the energy of a callow youth's.

Sherry turned and her gaze was trapped in Roarke's. At the tender look in his eyes, her breath wedged in her lungs, tightening her chest. Her heart thudded nervously.

"I guess I should go inside," she said, hardly recognizing her own voice.

Roarke nodded, willing her to leave him while he had the strength to resist her.

Sherry didn't move; her legs felt like mush and she sincerely doubted that they'd support her. If she budged at all, it was to lean closer to Roarke. Never in all her life had she wanted a man to hold her more. His gaze fell to her mouth and she moistened her lips in invitation, yearning for his kiss.

Roarke groaned inwardly and closed his eyes, but that only served to increase his awareness of her. She smelled of flowers, fresh and unbelievably sweet. Warmth radiated from her and he yearned to wrap his arms around her and feel for himself her incredible softness.

"Good night, Sherry," he said forcefully, bounding to his feet. "I'll see you in the morning."

Sherry sagged with relief and watched as Roarke marched away with the purposeful strides of a marine drill sergeant, his hands bunched into tight fists at his side.

Chapter Six

I demand that we form a search party," Wendy cried, crossing her arms over her chest and glaring at Sherry. "You did when Ralph was missing."

"Wendy, sweetheart," Sherry said, doing her best to keep calm. "Ralph is a living, breathing animal."

"A *rodent hamustro* actually," Sally informed them knowingly.

"Whatever. The thing is—a misplaced Ken doll doesn't take on the urgency of a missing rodent."

"But someone stole him."

Sherry refused to believe that any of the girls would want Ken badly enough to pilfer him from their cabin mate. "We'll keep looking, Wendy, but for now that's the best we can do."

Hands placed on her hips, the youngster surveyed the room, her eyes zeroing in on her peers. "All right, which one of you crooks kidnapped Ken-Richie?"

"Wendy!"

"I refuse to live in a den of thieves!"

"No one stole your doll," Sherry said for the tenth time. "I'm sure you misplaced him."

Wendy gave her a look of utter disgust. "No one in their right mind would misplace the one and only love of Barbie-Brenda's life."

"Oh, brother," Sherry muttered under her breath.

"I think Longfellow might have done it," Pamela inserted cautiously. "It's just the kind of thing a ghost would do."

"Longfellow?"

"Right," Jan and Jill chimed in eagerly. "Longfellow."

Wendy considered that for a moment, then agreed with an abrupt nod of her head and appeared to relax somewhat. "You know, I bet that's exactly what did happen."

Over the next two days the standard response to any problem was that Longfellow was responsible. Soon the entire camp was buzzing with tales of the make-believe ghost Sherry had invented.

"My mattress has more bumps than a camel," Gretchen claimed one morning.

Six preteens glanced at the chronic complainer and shouted in unison, "Longfellow did it!"

Ralph's cage door was left open to Pamela's dismay. "Longfellow," the girls informed her.

At breakfast, the Cream of Wheat had lumps. The girls looked at one another across the table, nodded once and cried, "Longfellow."

Every time Sherry heard Longfellow's name, she cringed inwardly. That Roarke hadn't heard about the friendly ghost was a miracle in itself. Sherry had already decided that when he did, she would give an Academy Award performance of innocence. By now, news of the spirit had infiltrated most of the cabins, although Sherry couldn't be certain which counselors had heard about him and who hadn't. She did notice, however, that the boys from Fred Spencer's cabin were unusually quiet about the ghost.

Since the night she'd met Roarke at the pay phone, their relationship had gone from a rocky, rut-filled road to a smooth-surfaced freeway. He'd shocked her by ordering coffee served at their early-morning meetings. Although he hadn't specifically said it was for her benefit, Sherry realized it was.

"I don't think I ever thanked you," she told him one morning early in the week, when the staff had been dismissed from their dawn session.

"Thanked me?" He looked up from reading over his notes.

"For the coffee." She gestured with the Styrofoam cup, her gaze holding his.

Roarke grinned and his smile alone had the power to set sail to her heart.

"If you'll notice, I haven't been late for a single meeting since the coffee arrived. Fact is, I don't even need to open my eyes. The alarm goes off, I dress in the dark and follow my nose to the staff room."

"I thought that would induce you to get here on time," he said, his gaze holding hers.

Actually, the coffee hadn't a single thing to do with it. She came because it was the only time of day she could count on seeing Roarke. Generally, they didn't have much cause to spend time with each other, because Roarke was busy with the running of the camp and Sherry had her hands full with her seven charges. That he'd become so important to her was something of a quandary for Sherry. The minute he discovered she'd falsified her references, she'd be discharged from Camp Gitche Gumee. More than

once Lynn had specifically told her that Mr. Roarke could
forgive anything but dishonesty. Sherry had trouble being
truthful with herself about her feelings for Roarke for fear
of what she'd discover.

"I'm pleased the coffee helped." Dragging his eyes away
from her, Roarke closed his notebook and walked out of
the building with her. "Have you spent much time star-
gazing lately?"

She shook her head and yawned. "Too tired."

"Pity," he mumbled softly.

It would have been so easy for Sherry to forget where
they were and who they were. She hadn't ever felt so
strongly attracted to a man. It was crazy! Sometimes she
wasn't completely sure she even liked him. Yet at all hours
of the day and night, she found herself fantasizing about
him. She imagined him taking her in his arms and kissing
her, and how firm and warm his mouth would feel over her
own. She dreamed about how good it would be to press her
head against his shoulder and lean on him, letting his
strength support her. She entertained fleeting fantasies
even while she was doing everything in her power to battle
the unreasonable desires.

"By the way," Roarke said, clearing his throat, "one of
the references you gave me came back marked 'no such
address.'"

"It did?" Sherry's heart pounded, stone-cold. She'd
prayed he wouldn't check, but knowing how thorough
Roarke was made that wish nothing short of stupid. She
was going to have to think of something, and quick.

"You must have listed the wrong address."

"Yes . . . I must have."

"When you've got a minute, stop off at the office and
you can check it over. I'll mail it out later."

"Okay."

They parted at the pay phone, Sherry heading toward her cabin and Roarke toward the mess hall.

The cabin was buzzing with activity when Sherry stepped inside, but when the girls spied their counselor the noise level dropped to a fading hum and the seven returned to their tasks much too smoothly.

Suspicious, Sherry paused and looked around not knowing exactly what she expected to find. The girls maintained a look of innocence until Sherry demanded, "What's going on here?"

"Nothing," Sally said, but she was smiling gleefully.

Sherry didn't believe it for a moment. "I don't trust you girls. What are you up to?" Her gaze swept the room. Never in her life had she seen more innocent-looking faces. "Ginny?" Sherry turned her questions to the teenager who replaced her in the early mornings when she attended the staff meetings.

"Don't look at me." The teenager slapped her sides, looking as blameless as the girls.

"Something's going on." Sherry didn't need to be a psychic to feel the vibrations in the air. The seven wizards were up to something, and whatever it was seemed to have drawn them together. All through breakfast they were congenial and friendly, leaning over to whisper secrets to one another. Not a single girl found fault with another. Not even Gretchen! Their eyes fairly sparkled with mischief.

Sherry studied them as they left the mess hall for their classes. Her group stayed together, looking at one another and giggling with impish delight without provocation.

"Hi." Lynn pulled out a bench and sat across the table from Sherry.

Sherry pulled her gaze away from her wizards. "How's it going?"

Lynn shrugged. "I'm not sure."

"Have you been seeing Peter?"

"Are you kidding?" Lynn asked and snorted softly. "We know better. Oh, we see each other all the time, but never alone."

"That's wise."

"Maybe, but it sure is boring." Lynn lifted her mug to her lips and downed her hot chocolate. "It's getting so bad that the eighth-grade boys are beginning to look good to me."

Despite the seriousness of her friend's expression, Sherry chuckled. "Now that's desperate."

"Peter and I know the minute we sneak off, we'll get caught—besides we aren't that stupid." She sagged against the back of her chair. "I don't know what it is, but Mr. Roarke has this sixth sense about these things. He always seems to know what's happening. Peter's convinced that Mr. Roarke is aware of everything that goes on between us."

"How could he be?"

Lynn shrugged. "Who knows? I swear that man is clairvoyant."

"I'm sure you're exaggerating." Sherry's stomach reacted with dread. She was living with a time bomb ticking away—she'd been a fool to have tried to slip something as important as references past Roarke.

"Since Peter and I haven't seen a lot of each other," Lynn continued, "we've been writing notes. It's not the same as being alone with each other, but it's been...I don't know...kind of neat to have his thoughts there to read over and over again."

Sherry's nod was absent.

"Well, I suppose I'd best get to work." Lynn swung her leg over the bench and stood.

"Right," Sherry returned, "work."

"By the way, I think the signs are cute."

Sherry's head shot up. "Signs? What signs?"

"The ones posted outside the cabins. How'd you ever get Mr. Roarke to agree to it? Knowing the way he feels about fairy tales, it's a wonder—"

Rarely had Sherry moved more quickly. She'd known her girls were up to something. Signs. Oh, good heavens! By the time she was outside the mess hall, she was able to view exactly what Lynn had been talking about. In front of each cabin a large picket had been driven into the ground that gave the cabin a name. The older boys' quarters was dubbed Pinocchio's Parlor, the younger Captain Hook's Hangout. Cinderella's Castle was saved for the older girls. But by far the largest and most ornate sign was in front of her own quarters. It read: The Home of Sherry White and the Seven Wizards.

The quality of the workmanship amazed Sherry. Each letter was perfectly shaped and printed in bright, bold colors. There wasn't any question that her girls were responsible, but she hadn't a clue as to when they'd had the time. It came to her then—they hadn't painted the markers themselves, but ordered them. Gretchen had claimed more than once that her father had given her her own American Express card. She'd flashed it a couple of times, wanting to impress the others. Of all the girls, Gretchen had taken hold of the tales of fantasy with rare enthusiasm. She loved them, and had devoured all the books Sherry had given her.

"Miss White," Roarke's voice boomed from across the lawn.

Her blood ran cold, but she did her best not to show her apprehension. "Yes?"

He pointed in the direction of his headquarters. "In my office. Now!"

The sharp tone of his voice stiffened Sherry's spine. If she'd been in a less vulnerable position, she would have clicked her heels, saluted crisply and marched toward him with her arms stiffly swinging at her sides. Now, however, was not the time to display any signs of resistance. She could recognize hot water when she saw it!

It seemed the entire camp came to a halt. Several children lingered outside the classrooms, gazing her way anxiously. Teachers found excuses to wander around the grounds, a few were in a cluster, pointing in Sherry's direction. Fred Spencer, the counselor who had made his opinion of Sherry's ideas well-known, looked on with a sardonic grin. Each group paused to view the unfolding scene with keen interest.

Before Sherry had a chance to move, Roarke was at her side. Over the past few weeks, she'd provoked the stubborn camp director more times than she could count, but never anything like what he suspected she'd done this time. A muscle worked its way along the side of Roarke's stern jaw, tightening his already harsh features.

"M-maybe it would be best to talk about this after you've had the opportunity to cool down and think matters through. I realize it looks bad, but—"

"We'll discuss it *now*."

"Roarke, I know you're going to have trouble believing this, but I honestly didn't have anything to do with those signs."

His lip curled sardonically. "Then who did?"

Sally and Gretchen hurried up behind the couple. "Don't be angry with Miss White," Gretchen called out righteously. "She told you the truth. In fact, the signs are a surprise to her, too."

"Then just who is responsible?" Roarke demanded.

The two youngsters looked at each other, grinned and shouted their announcement. "Longfellow!"

"Who?"

Sherry wished the ground would open so she could dive out of sight and escape before anyone noticed. If Roarke had frowned upon her filling the girls' heads with fairy tales as "romantic nonsense," then he was sure to disapprove of her creating a friendly spook.

"Longfellow's our ghost," Sally explained, looking surprised that the camp director wouldn't know about him. "Longfellow, you know—he lives here."

"Your what? Who lives where?" Roarke managed to keep his voice even, but the look he gave Sherry could have forced the world into another ice age.

"The ghost who lives at Camp Gitche Gumee," Sally continued patiently. "You mean, no one's ever told you about Longfellow?"

"Apparently not," Roarke returned calmly. "Who told *you* about him?"

"Miss White," the girls answered in unison, sealing Sherry's fate.

"I see."

Sherry winced at the sharpness in his voice, but the girls appeared undaunted—or else they hadn't noticed.

"You aren't upset with Miss White, are you?" Sally asked, her young voice laced with concern. "She's the best counselor we ever had."

"The signs really were Longfellow's idea," Gretchen added dryly.

Roarke made a show of looking at his watch. "Isn't it about time for your first class? Miss White and I will discuss this matter in private."

The children scurried off to their class, leaving Sherry to face Roarke's displeasure alone. Having two of her charges defend her gave her ego a boost. Roarke was so tall and overpowering that she realized, not for the first time, how easily he could intimidate her. A sense of consequence seemed to emanate from him, and something about his presence caused her to square her shoulders, thrust out her chin and face him head-on.

She turned to look at him, hands on her hips, feet braced. "I have other plans this morning. If you'll excuse me, I would—"

"The only place you're going is my office."

"So you can shout at me?"

"So we can discuss this senselessness," he said through gritted teeth.

It wouldn't do any good to argue. He turned and left her to follow him, and because she had no choice, she did as he requested, dreading the coming confrontation. For the past few days at camp, Sherry had come to hope that things would be better between her and Roarke. The night he'd walked her back from the pay phone had blinded her to the truth. They simply didn't view these children in the same way. Roarke saw them as miniature adults and preferred to treat them as such. Sherry wanted them to be children. The clash was instinctive and intense.

Roarke held the office door open for her and motioned with his hand for her to precede him. Sherry remembered what Lynn had said about Roarke firing people in the mornings. Well here she was, but she wasn't going down without an argument. Of all the things she had expected to be dismissed over—falsified references, misleading lesson plans, ghost stories—now it looked as if she was going to get the shaft for something she hadn't even done.

"I already told you I had nothing to do with the signs," she spoke first.

"Directly, that may be true, but indirectly there's no one more to blame."

Sherry couldn't argue with him there. She was the one who had introduced the subject to her seven wizards.

"If you recall, I specifically requested that you stop filling the children's heads with flights of fancy."

"I did," she cried.

"It's all too obvious that you didn't." His shoulders stiff, he marched around the desk and faced her. Leaning forward, he placed his hands on the desktop and glared in her direction. "You're one of those people who request an inch and take a mile."

"I..."

"In an effort to compromise, I've given you a free hand with the nine- and ten-year-old girls. Against my better judgment, I turned my head and ignored gin rummy taught in place of statistics classes. I looked the other way while you claimed to be studying frozen molecules when in reality you were sampling homemade ice cream."

"Don't you think I know that? Don't you think I appreciate it?"

"Obviously, you don't," he shouted, his voice gaining volume with each word. "Not if you stir up more problems by conjuring up a...a ghost. Of all the insane ideas you've come up with, this one takes the cake."

"Longfellow's not that kind of spook."

His eyes narrowed with a dark, furious frown. "I suppose you're going to tell me—"

"He's a friendly spirit."

Roarke muttered something she couldn't hear and raked a hand through his hair. "I can't believe I'm listening to this."

"The girls have a hundred complaints a day. Wendy's Ken-Richie doll is missing—one of the ten she brought to camp."

"Ken who?"

"Her Ken doll that she named Ken-Richie."

"What the hell is a Ken doll?"

"Never mind, that's not important."

"Anything you do is important because it leads to disaster."

"All right," Sherry cried, losing patience. "You want to know. Fine. Ken-Richie is the mate for Barbie-Brenda. Understand that?"

Roarke was growing more frustrated by the minute. There had been a time when he felt he had a grip on what was happening at camp, but from the minute Sherry had arrived with her loony ideas, everything had slid downhill.

"Anyway," Sherry continued, "it's so much easier to blame Longfellow for stealing Ken-Richie than to have a showdown among the girls."

"Who actually took the...doll?"

"Oh, I don't know—no one does. That's the point. But I'm sure he'll turn up sooner or later."

"Do you actually believe this...Longfellow will bring him back?" Roarke taunted.

"Exactly."

"That's pure nonsense."

"To you, maybe, but you're not a kid and you're not a counselor."

"No, I'm the director of this camp, and I want this stupidity stopped. Now."

Sherry clamped her mouth closed.

"Is that understood, Miss White?"

"I can't."

"What do you mean you can't? You have my direct order."

She lifted her palms and shrugged her shoulders. "It's gone too far. Almost everyone in the entire camp knows about Longfellow now. I can't put a stop to the children talking about him."

Roarke momentarily closed his eyes. "Do you realize what you've done?"

"But it was all in fun."

He ignored that. "This camp has a reputation for academic excellence."

"How can a make-believe ghost ruin that?"

"If you have to ask, then we're in worse trouble than I thought."

Sherry threw up her hands in disgust. "Oh, honestly!"

"This is serious."

Now it was Sherry's turn to close her eyes and gain control of her temper. She released a drawn-out sigh. "What is it you want me to do?" she asked, keeping her voice as unemotional as possible. "I realize that within a few weeks, I've managed to ruin the reputation for excellence of this camp—"

"I didn't say that," he countered sharply.

"By all rights I should be tossed out of here on my ear...."

Roarke raised both hands to stop her. They glared at each other, each daring the other to speak first. "Before this conversation heats up any more, I think we should both take time to cool down," Roarke said stiffly.

Sherry met his gaze defiantly, her heart slamming against her breast with dread. "Do you want me to leave?"

He hesitated, then nodded. "Maybe that would be best."

Tears burned the backs of her eyes and her throat grew tight with emotion. "I'll...pick up my check this afternoon."

Roarke frowned. "I want us to cool our tempers—I'm not firing you."

Sherry's head snapped up and her heart soared with hopeful expectation. Roarke wasn't letting her go! She felt like a prisoner who'd been granted a death row pardon by the governor at the last minute. "But it's morning—you mean, you don't want me to leave Camp Gitche Gumee?"

Roarke looked confused. "Of course not. What are you talking about?"

The flood of relief that washed over her submerged her in happiness. It took everything within Sherry not to toss her arms around his neck and thank him.

With as much aplomb as she could muster, she nodded, turned around and walked across the floor, but paused when she reached the door. "Thank you," she whispered, sincerely grateful.

It seemed the entire camp was waiting for her. A hush fell across the campus when she appeared. Faces turned in her direction and Lynn gestured with her hands, wanting to know the outcome.

Sherry smiled in response, and it seemed that everyone around released an elongated sigh. All except Fred Spencer, who Sherry suspected would be glad to see her leave. Until that moment, Sherry hadn't realized how many friends she'd made in her short stay at Camp Gitche Gumee. Her legs felt weak, her arms heavy. Although she'd been fortunate enough to hold on to her job, Roarke was still furious with her. More than anything she wanted to remain here for the entire camp session. And not be-

cause she was running away from Phyliss, either. She'd left
Seattle because of her crazy, wonderful stepmother, seeking a respite from the woman she loved and didn't wish to
offend. But Sherry wanted to stay in California for entirely different reasons. Some of which she sensed she
didn't fully understand herself.

At break time, Sally, Gretchen and two other girls came
storming into the cabin.

"Hi," Sherry said cheerfully. "What are you guys doing
here?"

The girls exchanged meaningful glances. "Nothing,"
Wendy said, swinging her arms and taking small steps
backward.

"We just wanted to be sure everything was okay."

Sherry's answering grin was wide. She winked and
whispered, "Things couldn't be better."

"Good!" A breathless Jan and Jill arrived to chime in
unison.

Producing a stern look was difficult, but Sherry managed. She pinched her lips together and frowned at her
young charges. The last thing she needed was to do something else to irritate Roarke. "Aren't you girls supposed to
be in class?"

"Yes, but . . ."

"But we wanted to see what happened to you."

"It's too hot to sit inside a classroom, anyway,"
Gretchen grumbled.

"Gretchen's right," Sally added, looking surprised to
agree with the complainer.

"Scat," Sherry cried, "before I reach for my machine
gun."

The girls let loose with a shriek of mock terror and ran
from the cabin, down the steps and across the lawn. Sherry

grinned as she watched them scatter like field mice before a prowling cat.

It was then that she noticed the signs in front of each cabin had been removed. She crossed her arms, leaned against the doorjamb and experienced a twinge of regret. Cinderella's Castle was far more original than Cabin Three, even Roarke had to admit that.

After such shaky beginnings, the morning progressed smoothly. Sherry dressed to work out in the exercise room, then ate lunch with the girls, who chatted easily. Sherry took a couple of minutes to joke about the signs, hoping to reassure them that everything was fine. But she didn't mention Longfellow, although the name of the make-believe ghost could be heard now and again from various tables around the mess hall.

Throughout the meal, Sherry had only a fleeting look at Roarke. He came in, made his announcements and joined the teachers at their table for the noontime meal. He spoke to several counselors, but went out of his way to avoid Sherry, she noted. She hadn't expected him to seek her out for conversation, but she didn't appreciate being ignored, either.

Following lunch, Sherry slipped into the exercise room. Ginny was already there working out with the weights.

"Hi," the young assistant greeted, revealing her pleasure at seeing Sherry.

"Hi," Sherry returned, climbing onto the stationary bicycle and inserting her feet into the stirrups. Pedaling helped minimize the effects of all the fattening food she was consuming at camp.

Ginny, strapping a five-pound belt around her own waist, studied Sherry. "You should wear weights if you expect the biking to do any good."

"No thanks," Sherry said with a grin. "I double-knot my shoelaces; that's good enough."

The teenager laughed. "I heard you had a run-in with Mr. Roarke this morning. How'd you make out?"

"All right, I suppose." Sherry would rather let the subject drop with that. The events of the morning were best forgotten.

"From what I heard, he's been on the warpath all day."

"Oh?" She didn't want to encourage the teenager to gossip, but on the other hand, she was curious to discover what had been happening.

"Apparently one of the kids got caught doing something and was sent into Mr. Roarke's office. When Mr. Roarke questioned him, the boy said Longfellow made him do it. Isn't that the ghost you told the girls about not so long ago?"

Sherry's feet went lax while the wheel continued spinning. Oh dear, this just wasn't going to be her day.

"Something else must have happened, too, because he looked as mad as a hornet right before lunch."

Sherry had barely had time to assimilate that when Lynn appeared in the doorway, her young face streaked with tears.

"Lynn, what happened?"

Sherry's friend glanced at Ginny and wiped the tears from her pale cheek. "Can we talk alone?"

"Sure." Sherry immediately stopped pedaling and climbed off the bike. She placed her arm around the younger girl's shoulders. "Tell me what's upset you so much."

"I-it's Mr. Roarke."

"Yes," she coaxed.

"He found some of the notes I'd written to Peter. He wants to talk to us first thing in the morning...the morning—we both know what that means. I...I think we're both going to be fired."

Chapter Seven

Sherry woke at the sound of the alarm and lay with her eyes open, savoring the dream. She'd been in a rowboat with Roarke in the middle of the lake. The oars had skimmed the water as he lazily paddled over the silver water. Everything was different between them. Everything was right. All their disagreements had long since been settled. The pros and cons of a friendly ghost named Longfellow were immaterial. All that mattered was the two of them together.

The looks they'd shared as the water lapped gently against the side of the small boat reminded Sherry of the evening they'd sat on the porch and gazed into the brilliant night sky. Stars were in Sherry's eyes in her dream, too, but Jeff Roarke had put them there.

With a melancholy sigh, she tossed aside the covers and sat on the edge of the mattress. It was silly to be so affected by a mere dream, but it had been so real and so wonderful. However, morning brought with it the chill of reality, and Sherry was concerned for Lynn and Peter. She had to think of some way to help them.

After dressing, she held in a yawn and walked across the thick lawn to the staff room. Her arms were crisscrossed over her ribs, but Sherry couldn't decide if it was to ward off a morning chill or the truth that awaited her outside her dreamworld. Birds chirped playfully in the background and the sun glimmered through the tall timbers, casting a pathway of shimmering light across the dewy grass, giving Sherry hope.

At the staff room, Sherry discovered that only a couple of the other counselors had arrived. Roarke was there, standing at the podium in the front, flipping through his notes.

With the warm sensations of the dream lingering in her mind, Sherry approached him, noted his frown and waited for him to acknowledge her before she spoke. Uncomfortable seconds passed and still Roarke didn't raise his head. When he did happen to look up, his gaze met hers, revealing little. Sherry realized that he hadn't forgotten their heated discussion. He'd been the one to suggest that they delay talking because things were getting out of hand. But from the narrowed, sharp appraisal he gave her it was all too apparent that his feelings ran as hot today as they had the day before.

"Miss White." He said her name stiffly.

Sherry grimaced at the chill in his voice. "Good morning."

He returned her greeting with an abrupt nod and waited. There had never been a woman who angered Roarke more than Sherry White. This thing with the ghost she'd invented infuriated him to the boiling point, and he'd been forced to ask her to leave his office yesterday for fear of what more he'd say or do. His anger had been so intense that he'd wanted to shake her. *Wrong,* his mind tossed back—it had taken every ounce of determination he possessed, which was considerable, not to pull her into his arms and kiss some common sense into her.

The power she had to jostle his secure, impenetrable existence baffled him. He'd never wanted a woman with the intensity that he wanted Sherry, and the realization was frightening. A full day had passed since their last encounter, and he still wasn't in complete control of his emotions. Even with all this time to cool his temper, she caused his blood to boil in his veins.

No other counselor had been granted the latitude he'd given her. He'd turned a blind eye to her other schemes, accepting lesson plans that stated she would be teaching a study on centrifugal force when he knew she was planning on cooking popcorn. The evening sessions weren't the only rule he'd stretched on her behalf. The other counselors would question the integrity of his leadership if they knew about Ralph. But the ghost—now that was going too far. The truth about Longfellow had driven him over the edge. She'd abused his willingness to adapt to her creativity and in the process infuriated him.

Although his emotions were muddled, no woman had intrigued him the way Sherry did, either. He couldn't seem to get her out of his mind. He had enough problems organizing this camp without entertaining romantic thoughts about one impertinent counselor.

"You wanted something?" he asked, forcing his voice to remain cool and unemotional.

"Yes…you said yesterday that you thought it'd be best if we continued our discussion later."

Roarke glanced at his watch. "There's hardly time now."

"I didn't mean this minute exactly," Sherry answered. He was making this more difficult than necessary.

"Is there something you'd like to say?"

"Yes."

"Then this afternoon would be convenient," Roarke said coldly. He might be agreeing to another meeting, he told himself, but he couldn't see what they had left to say. He'd been angry, true, but not completely unreasonable. Nothing she could say would further her cause.

Sherry tried to smile, but the effort was too much for her. "I'll be there about one o'clock."

"That would be fine."

By now the small room was filled to capacity, and she walked to the back, looking for a chair. Lynn had saved her a seat, and Sherry sank down beside her friend, disappointed and uncomfortable. Twenty minutes into the day and already her dream was shattered. So much for lingering looks and meaningful gazes. She might as well be made of mud for all the interest Jeff Roarke showed her.

The announcements were dealt with quickly, but before Roarke could continue, Fred Spencer, the counselor for the older boys, raised his hand.

"Fred, you had a question?"

"Yes." Fred stood and loudly cleared his throat. "There's been talk all over camp about Longfellow. Who or what is he?"

Sherry scooted so far down in her chair that she was in danger of slipping right onto the floor. Fred Spencer was a royal pain in the rear end as far as Sherry was concerned.

"Longfellow is a friendly ghost," Roarke explained wryly. "As I understand it, he derived his name from Henry Wadsworth Longfellow, the poet."

Still Fred remained standing. "A ghost?" he shouted. "And just whose idea was this nonsense?" A hum of raised voices followed, some offended, others amused. "Why I've heard of nothing else for the past twenty-four hours. It's Longfellow this, Longfellow that. The least bit of confusion with kids can become a major catastrophe. These children come to this camp to learn responsibility. They're not gaining a darn thing by placing the blame on an imaginary spirit."

Unable to endure any more, Sherry sprang to her feet. "I believe you're putting too much emphasis on a trivial matter. The camp is visited by a friendly ghost. It doesn't need to be made into a big deal. Longfellow is for fun. The children aren't frightened by him, and he adds a sense of adventure to the few weeks they're here."

"Trivial," Fred countered, turning to face Sherry with his hands placed defiantly on his hips. "I've had nothing but problems from the moment this...this Longfellow was mentioned."

"Sit down, Fred," Roarke said, taking control.

Fred ignored the request. "I suppose you're responsible for this phantom ghost, Miss White? Just like you were with those ridiculous signs?"

Sherry opened and closed her mouth. "Yes, I invented Longfellow."

"I thought as much," Fred announced with profound righteousness.

Again the conversational hum rose from the other staff members, the group quickly taking sides. From bits and pieces of conversations that Sherry heard, the room appeared equally divided. Some saw no problem with Longfellow while others were uncertain. Several made comments about liking Sherry's style, but others agreed with Fred.

Roarke slammed his fist against the podium. "Mr. Spencer, Miss White, I would greatly appreciate it if you would take your seats."

Fred sat, but he didn't remain silent. "I demand that we put an end to this ghost nonsense."

A muscle in Roarke's jaw twitched convulsively and his gaze lifted to meet and hold Sherry's. "I'm afraid it's too late for that. Word of Longfellow is out now, and any effort to do away with him would only encourage the children."

Grumbling followed, mostly from Fred Spencer and his cronies.

"My advice is to ignore him and hope that everyone will forget the whole thing," Roarke spoke above the chatter.

"What about Miss White?" Fred demanded. "She's been nothing but a worry from the moment she arrived. First those ridiculous signs and now this. Where will it end?"

"That's not true," Lynn shouted, and soared to her feet in an effort to defend her friend. She gripped the back of the chair in front of her and glared at the older man. "Sherry's been great with the kids!"

"Miss Duffy, kindly sit down," Roarke barked, raising his hands to quiet the room. The noise level went down appreciably, although the controversy appeared far from settled. He spoke to Fred Spencer with enough authority to quickly silence the other man. "This is neither the time nor the place to air our differences of opinion regarding another counselor's teaching methods."

Sherry wasn't fooled. Roarke wasn't defending her so much as protecting the others from criticism should Fred take exception to another's techniques. Fred Spencer's reputation as a complainer was as well-known as Gretchen's.

"If the staff can't speak out, then exactly whose job is it?" Fred shouted.

"Mine!" Roarke declared, and the challenge in his voice was loud and infinitely clear.

"Good, then I'll leave the situation in your hands."

From her position, Sherry could see that Fred wasn't appeased. Nor did she believe he would quietly drop the subject. From the beginning, she'd known he disagreed with her efforts with the children. Whenever he had the chance, he put down her ideas and found reason to criticize her.

The remainder of the meeting passed quickly, but not fast enough as far as Sherry was concerned. She and Lynn walked out of the staff room together.

"I can't believe that man," Lynn grumbled. "His idea of having fun is watching paint dry."

"Miss Duffy."

Roarke's cold voice stopped both women. The teenager cast a pleading glance at Sherry before turning around to face her employer.

"I believe we have an appointment."

"Oh, yes," Lynn said with a wan smile. "I forgot."

"I'm afraid that's part of the problem," Roarke returned with little humor. "You seem to be forgetting several things lately."

Sherry opened her mouth to dilute his sarcasm, but one piercing glare from Roarke silenced her. This wasn't her business. She didn't want to say or do anything to irritate him any more. Her greatest fear was that after the events of the morning, Roarke wasn't in any mood to deal kindly with Lynn and Peter. With a heavy heart, Sherry returned to her cabin.

Ginny had roused the girls and there was the typical mad confusion of morning. As usual there was fighting over the bathroom and how long Jan and Jill hogged the mirror to braid each other's hair.

"My mattress has got more lumps than the Cream of Wheat we had the other day," Gretchen muttered, sitting on the side of the bed and rubbing the small of her back.

Pamela was stroking Ralph's head with one finger inserted between the bars of the cage; both girl and rodent appeared content.

Sally and Wendy were already dressed, eager to start another day, while Diane slumbered, resisting all wake-up notices.

Sherry walked over to the sleeping youngster's bunk and pulled out the Hardy Boys novel and flashlight from beneath her pillow. Once she'd turned the ten-year-old on to Judy Blume, Beverly Cleary and other preteen series books, there had been no stopping her. Diane's favorite had turned out to be John D. Fitzgerald's Great Brain books. The dry textbook material had been replaced by fiction, and a whole new world had opened up to the little girl. Now Sherry had to teach Diane about moderation. "Sleeping Beauty," she coaxed softly, "rise and shine."

"Go away," Diane moaned. "I'm too tired."

"Ken-Richie hasn't shown up yet," Wendy muttered disparagingly. "I wonder if Longfellow's ever going to bring him back." She might have mentioned the ghost, but her narrowed gaze surveyed the room, accusing each one who was unlucky enough to fall prey to her eagle eye.

"Hey, don't look at me," Sally shouted. "I wouldn't take your stupid Ken-Richie if someone paid me. *Batrachoseps attenuatus* are my thing."

"What?" Gretchen demanded.

"The California Slender Salamander," Wendy informed her primly. "If you were really so smart you'd know that."

"I'm not into creepy crawly things the way you are."

"I noticed."

"If my American Express card can't buy it, I don't want it," Gretchen informed her primly.

"It's nearly breakfast time," Sally encouraged Diane, roughly shaking the other girl's shoulder. "And Wednesday's French toast day."

"I don't want to eat," Diane murmured on the tail end of a yawn. "I'd rather sleep."

"Listen, kiddo," Sherry said, bending low and whispering in the reluctant girl's ear, "either you're up and dressed in ten minutes flat, or I won't loan you the other books in the Hardy Boys series."

Diane's dark brown eyes flew open. "Okay, okay, I'm awake."

"Here." Sally handed her a pair of shorts and matching top and Sherry looked on approvingly. The girls were developing rich friendships this summer. Even Gretchen, with her constant complaining and her outrageous bragging, had mellowed enough to find a friend or two. She still found lots of things that needed to be brought to Sherry's attention, like lumpy mattresses and the dangers of sleeping too close to the window. Her credit card was flashed for show when her self-worth needed a boost, but all in all, Gretchen had turned into a decent kid.

Feeling sentimental, Sherry looked around at the group of girls she'd been assigned and felt her heart compress with affection. These seven little wizards had securely tucked themselves into the pocket of her heart. She would long remember them. The girls weren't all she'd recall about this summer, though. Memories of Roarke would always be with her. Her stay at the camp was nearly half over and already she dreaded leaving, knowing it was doubtful that she'd see Roarke again. The thought brought with it a brooding sense of melancholy. For all their differences, she'd come to appreciate him and his efforts at the camp.

Much to Sherry's surprise, and probably Fred Spencer's too, the occupants of Cabin Two arrived in the dining hall precisely on time without stragglers. French toast was a popular breakfast, and when the girls had finished, Pam slipped Sherry an extra piece of the battered bread and asked if she would feed it to Ralph.

"Sure," Sherry assured the child. "But I'll tell him it's from you."

The blue eyes brightened. "He likes you, too, Miss White."

"And I think he's a great mascot for our cabin," she admitted in a whisper.

Once the mess hall had emptied, Sherry poured herself a steaming cup of coffee and paused to savor the first sip. She had just raised the cup to her lips when Lynn entered the room, paused to look around and, seeing Sherry, hurried across the floor.

"How'd it go?"

Lynn bit her lower lip and dejectedly shook her head. "Not good, but then I didn't expect it would with Mr. Roarke in such a lousy mood."

"He didn't fire you, did he?"

"I'm afraid so."

"But..." Sherry was so outraged she could barely speak. She hadn't believed he'd do something so unfair. True, the two had broken camp rules, but so had she, so had everyone. It wasn't as though Lynn and Peter were overtly carrying on a torrid romance. No one was aware that they cared for each other. If Roarke hadn't found their notes, he wouldn't even have known they were interested in each other.

"I have to pack my bags," Lynn said calmly, but her voice cracked, relaying her unhappiness. "But before I go I just wanted to tell you how much I enjoyed working with you." Tears briefly glistened in the other girl's eyes.

Flustered and angry, Sherry ran her fingers through her hair and sadly shook her head. "I don't believe this."

"He was upset, partly because of what happened this morning, I think, and other problems. There's a lot more to being camp director than meets the eye."

Sherry wasn't convinced she would have been so gracious with Roarke had their circumstances been reversed.

"Listen," Sherry said and braced her hands against her friend's shoulders. "Let me talk to him. I might be able to help."

"It won't do any good," Lynn argued. "I've never known Mr. Roarke to change his mind."

While chewing on her lower lip, a plan of action began to form in Sherry's befuddled mind. Sure, she could storm into Roarke's office and demand an explanation, but they'd just end up in another shouting match. As the camp director, he would no doubt remind her that whom he chose to fire or hire was none of her concern. The risk was too great, since he could just as easily dismiss her. Following the events of the past few days, she would be cooking her own goose to openly challenge him.

Her plan was better. Much better.

"Don't pack yet," Sherry said slowly, thoughtfully.

"What do you mean?"

"Just that. Go to your quarters and wait for me there."

"Sherry—" Lynn's brow creased with a troubled frown "—what do you have in mind? You don't look right. Listen, Mr. Roarke isn't having a good day—I don't think this would be the time to talk to him." Lynn paused, set her teeth to chewing at the corner of her mouth and sighed. "At least tell me what you have in mind."

Sherry shook her head, not wanting to answer in case her scheme flopped. "Don't worry. I'll get back to you as soon as possible."

"Okay," Lynn agreed reluctantly.

Sherry headed directly to Roarke's office, knocking politely.

"Yes."

Sherry let herself inside. "Hello."

He hesitated, then raised his pen from the paper. This morning was quickly going from bad to worse. He'd been angry when he'd talked to Lynn and Peter. Angry and unreasonable. He'd dismissed them both unfairly and had since changed his mind. Already, he'd sent a message to the two to return to his office. He never used to doubt his decisions. Everything had been cut-and-dried. Black or white. Simple, uncomplicated. And then Sherry had tumbled into his peaceful existence with all the agility of a circus clown, and nothing had been the same since. He wanted to blame her for his dark mood. She occupied his mind night and day. Fiona was insipid tea compared to Sherry's sparkling champagne.

Sherry tempted him to the limit of his control. A simple smile left him weak with the longing to hold her in his arms. The energy it required for him to keep his hands off her was driving him crazy and weakening him. The situation between them was impossible, and his anger with Lynn and Peter had been magnified by his own level of frustration. And here she was again.

"Is there something I can do for you, Miss White?"

Her steady gaze held his. "I came to apologize."

"What have you done this time?"

His attitude stung her ego, but Sherry swallowed down her indignation and continued calmly. "Nothing new, let me assure you."

"That's a relief."

Her hand touched the chair. "Would you mind if I sat down?"

Pointedly, he glanced at his watch. "If you insist."

Sherry did, claiming the chair. "Things haven't gone very smoothly between us lately, have they?" she began in an even, controlled voice. "I decided that perhaps it would be best if we cleared the air."

"If it's about Longfellow—"

"No," she interrupted, then sadly shook her head. "It's more than that."

For several moments, he was silent, giving Sherry time to compose her thoughts. She'd come on Lynn and Peter's behalf, yearning to turn circumstances so he would rehire the two teenagers. That had been her original intention, but now that she was in his office, she couldn't go through with it. What she felt for this man was real, and their minor differences were quickly forming a chasm between them that might never be spanned unless she took the first leap. She turned her palms up and noted that his hard-sculpted features had relaxed. "I'm not even sure where to start."

"Miss White—"

"Sherry," she cried in frustration. "My name is Sherry and you damn well know it." Abruptly, she made a move to stand, her hands braced on the chair arms. "And this is exactly what I'm talking about. I don't call you Mr. Roarke, yet you insist upon addressing me formally, as if I were...I don't know, some stiff, starched counselor so unbending that I refuse anyone the privilege of using my name."

Roarke's gaze widened with her outburst. "You came to apologize?" He made the statement a question, confused by her irrational behavior. Sherry was too gutsy to be ambivalent. Whatever it was she had to say was real enough to sincerely trouble her.

"That was my original thought," she said, standing now and facing him. "But I'm not sure anymore. All I know is that I want things to be different between us."

"Different?"

"Yes," she cried, "every day, it seems, there's something that I've done to displease you. You can't even look at me anymore without frowning. I don't want to be a thorn in your side or a constant source of irritation."

"Sherry—"

"Thank you," she murmured, interrupting him with a soft smile. "I feel a thousand times better just having you say my name."

The frown worrying Roarke's brow relaxed, and a slow, sensuous smile transformed his harsh features. "Although I may not have said it, I've always thought of you as Sherry."

"But you called me Miss White."

"The others..."

Briefly, she dropped her eyes, remembering Fred Spencer's dislike of her. "I know."

"I haven't been angry with you; it's just that circumstances have been working against us."

"I realize I haven't exactly made things easier."

Sherry didn't know the half of it, Roarke thought. At least once a day he'd been placed in the uncomfortable position of having to defend her from the jealousy and resentment of some of the others. But she was by far the most popular counselor in camp, and neither he nor anyone else was in any position to argue her success.

"I know, too," she continued, "that you've turned your head on more than one occasion while I've bent the rules and disrupted this camp."

"Bent the rules," he repeated with a soft laugh. "You've out-and-out pulverized them."

Sherry sighed with relief; she felt a hundred times better to be here with him, talking as they once had in the moonlight. How fragile that truce had been. Now, if possible, she wanted to strengthen that.

"It's important to me, Roarke—no matter what happens at camp—that we always remain friends."

Looking at her now, with the sunlight streaming through her chestnut hair, her dark eyes imploring his, searing their way through the thickest of resolves, it wasn't in Roarke to refuse her anything.

"You can be angry with me," she said. "God knows I give you plenty of reasons, but I have to feel deep down that as long as we share a foundation of mutual respect it won't matter. You could call me Miss White until the year 2000 and it wouldn't bother me, because inside I'd know."

Roarke was convinced she had no idea how lovely she was. Beautiful. Intelligent. Witty. Fun. He felt like a boy trapped inside on a rainy day. She was laughter and sunshine, and he'd never wanted a woman as badly as he did her at this moment.

He stood and moved to her side. Her gaze narrowed with doubt when he placed his hands on her shoulders and turned her to face him. "Just friends?" he asked softly, wanting so much more. After the first week he'd thought to send her straight back to Seattle, because in a matter of only a few days, she'd managed to disturb his orderly life and that of the entire camp. He hadn't. Her candor and wit had thrown him off balance. But staring at her now, he realized her eyes disturbed him far more. She had beautiful, soulful eyes that could search his face as though she were doing a study of his very heart.

Sherry's palms were flattened against Roarke's hard chest; her head tilted back to question the look in his eyes. Surely she was reading more than was there—yet what she saw caused her heartbeat to soar. "Roarke?" she questioned softly, uncertain.

"I want to be more than friends," he answered her, lowering his mouth to hers. "Much more than friends."

Her lips parted under his, warm and moist, eager and curious. For weeks, she'd hungered to feel Roarke's arms around her and experience the taste of his kiss. Now that she was cradled securely in his embrace, the sensation of supreme rightness burned through her. It was as though she'd waited all her life for exactly this moment, for exactly this man.

His arms tightened around her slender frame as he deepened the kiss, his mouth moving hungrily over hers, insistently shaping her lips with his own. Roarke's spirit soared and his heart sang. She'd challenged him, argued with him, angered him. And he loved her, truly loved her. For the first time in his life, he was head over heels in love. He'd thought himself exempt from the emotion, but meeting Sherry had convinced him otherwise.

"Sherry," he groaned. His hands pushing the hair back from her face, he spread eager kisses over her face.

Sherry's world was spinning and she slid her hands up his chest to circle his neck, clinging to the very thing that caused her world to career out of control. She was irrevocably lost in a haze of longing.

Roarke groaned as she fit her body snugly to his. His mouth crushed hers, sliding insistently back and forth, seducing her with his moist lips until hers parted, inviting the plunder of his tongue into the soft recesses of her mouth.

Sherry thought she'd die with wanting Roarke. He tore his lips from hers and held her as though he planned never to let her go. His arms crushed her, but she experienced no pain. Physical limitation prevented her from being any closer, and still she wasn't content, seeking more. His arms were wrapped around her waist, locked at the small of her back. She rotated her hips once, seeking a way to satisfy this incredible longing.

"Sherry, love," he groaned, "don't."

"Roarke, oh, Roarke, is this real?"

"More real than anything I've ever known," he answered, after a long moment.

She moved once more and he moaned, drew in a deep, audible breath and held it so long that she wondered if he planned ever to breathe again.

Raising her hands, she lovingly stroked his handsome face. "I feel like I could cry." She pressed her forehead to his chest. "I'm probably not making the least bit of sense."

Gently, he kissed the crown of her head. "I've wanted to hold you forever."

"Roarke," she said solemnly, raising her eyes to meet his. Her heart was shining through her gaze. "You can't fire Lynn and Peter. Please reconsider."

The words were like a knife ripping into his soul. Roarke released Sherry and stepped back with such abruptness that she staggered a step. "Is that what this is all about?"

Her eyes mirrored her bewilderment. "No, of course not," she murmured, but she couldn't meet the accusing doubt in his eyes. "Originally I came because Lynn told me you'd dismissed both her and Peter, but . . ."

"So you thought that if you could get me to kiss you, I'd change my mind."

That was so close to the truth that Sherry yearned to find a hole, curl up in it and magically disappear. The words to explain how everything had changed once she'd arrived at his office died on her lips. It would do no good to deny the truth; Roarke read her far too easily for her to try to convince him otherwise.

She didn't need to say a word for him to read the truth revealed in her eyes. "I see," he said, his voice heavy with rancor.

Sherry flinched. She had to try to explain or completely lose him. "Roarke, please listen. I may have thought that at first, but . . ."

The loud knock against the door stopped her.

His face had become as hard as stone and just as implacable. "If you'll excuse me, I have business to attend to."

"No," she cried, "at least give me a chance to explain."

"There's nothing more to say." He walked across the room and opened the door.

Lynn and Peter stood on the other side. Instantly Lynn's gaze flew to Sherry, wide and questioning.

"Come in," Roarke instructed, holding open the door. "Miss White was just leaving."

Arching her back, Sherry moved past Peter. As Sherry neared Lynn, the other girl whispered, "Your plan must have worked."

"It worked all right—even better than she dared hope," Roarke answered for her with a look of such contempt that Sherry longed to weep.

Chapter Eight

Sherry, I'm sorry," Lynn said for the tenth time that day. "I didn't think Mr. Roarke could hear me."

Sherry's feet pedaled the stationary bike all the more vigorously. She'd hoped that taking her frustration out on the exercise bike would lessen the ache in her heart. She should have known better. "Don't worry about it. What's done is done."

"But Mr. Roarke hasn't spoken to you in a week."

"I'll survive." But just barely, she mused. When he was through being angry, they'd talk, but from the look of things it could be some time before he'd cooled down enough to reason matters through. There was less than a month left of camp as it was. For seven, long, tedious days, Roarke had gone out of his way to avoid her. If she were in the same room, he found something important to distract him. At the staff meetings, he didn't call upon her unless absolutely necessary and said "Miss White" with such cool disdain that he might as well have stabbed a hot needle straight through her heart.

By the sheer force of her pride, Sherry had managed to hold her head high, but there wasn't a staff member at Camp Gitche Gumee who wasn't aware that Sherry White had fallen from grace. Fred Spencer was ecstatic and thrived on letting smug remarks drop when he suspected there was no one else around to hear. Without Roarke to support her ideas, Fred was given free rein to ridicule her suggestions. Not a single thing she'd campaigned for all week had made it past the fiery tongue of her most ardent opponent.

When Sherry proposed a sing-along at dusk, Fred argued that such nonsense would cut into the cabin's evening lessons. Roarke neither agreed nor disagreed, and the suggestion was quickly dropped. When she'd proposed organized hikes for the study of wildflowers, there had been some enthusiasm, until Fred and a few others countered that crowding too many activities into the already heavy academic schedule could possibly overextend the counselors and the children. A couple debated the issue on Sherry's behalf, but in the long run the idea was abandoned for lack of interest. Again Roarke remained stoically silent.

"Maybe you'll survive," Lynn said, breathing heavily as she continued her sit-ups, "but I don't know about the rest of us."

"Roarke hasn't been angry or unreasonable." Sherry was quick to defend him, although he probably wouldn't have appreciated it.

"No, it's much worse than that," Lynn said with a tired sigh.

"How do you mean?"

"If you'd been here last year, you'd notice the difference. It's like he's built a wall around himself and is closing everybody off. He used to talk to the kids a lot, spend time with them. I think he's hiding."

"Hiding?" Sherry prompted.

"Right." Lynn sat upright and folded her arms around her bent knees, resting her chin there. "If you want the truth, I think Mr. Roarke has fallen for you, only he's too proud to admit it."

Sherry's feet pumped harder, causing the wheel to whirl and hiss. A lump thickened in her throat. "I wish that were true."

"Look at the way he's making himself miserable and, consequently, everyone else. He's responsible for the morale of this camp, and for the past week or so there's been a thundercloud hanging over us all."

To disagree would be to lie. Lynn was right; the happy atmosphere of the camp had cooled decidedly. As for Roarke caring, it was more than Sherry dared hope. She wanted to believe it, but she sincerely doubted that he'd allow a misunderstanding to grow to such outrageous proportions if he did.

"Have you tried talking to him?" Lynn said next. "It couldn't hurt, you know."

Maybe not, but Jeff Roarke wasn't the only one with a surplus of pride. Sherry possessed a generous portion of the emotion herself.

"Well?" Lynn demanded when Sherry didn't respond. "Have you even tried to tell him your side of it?"

The door to the exercise room opened, and both women turned their attention to the tall, muscular man who stepped inside the room.

"Roarke," Sherry murmured. Her feet stopped pumping, but the rear wheel continued to spin.

He was dressed in faded gray sweatpants and a T-shirt, a towel draped around his neck. Just inside the door, he paused, looked around and frowned.

"Here's your chance," Lynn whispered, struggling to her feet. "Go for it, girl." She gave Sherry the thumbs-up sign and casually sauntered from the room, whistling a cheery tune as she went.

Sherry groaned inwardly; Lynn couldn't have been any more obvious had she openly announced that she was leaving to give the two time to sort out their myriad differences. Sherry nearly shouted for her to come back. Talking to Roarke in his present frame of mind would do no good.

While continuing to pedal, Sherry cast an anxious look in Roarke's direction. He ignored her almost as completely as she strove to ignore him. Lifting the towel from his neck he tossed it over the abdominal board of the weight gym and turned his back to her. The T-shirt followed the towel and he proceeded to go about bench-pressing a series of weights.

Without meaning to watch him, Sherry unwillingly found her gaze wandering over to him until it was all she could do to keep from staring outright. The muscles across his wide shoulders rippled with each movement, displaying the lean, hard build.

The inside of Sherry's mouth went dry; just watching him was enough to intoxicate her senses. His biceps bulged with each push.

The bike wheel continued to spin, but Sherry had long since given up pedaling. She freed her feet from the stirrups and climbed off. Her legs felt shaky, but whether it was from the hard exercise or from being alone with Roarke, Sherry couldn't tell.

"Hello," she said, in a voice that sounded strange even to her own ears. Nonchalantly, she removed the helmet with the tiny side mirror from her head. "I suppose you're wondering why I'd wear a helmet when I'm pedaling a stationary bike," she said, hoping to make light conversation.

Sweat broke out across Roarke's brow, but it wasn't from the exertion of lifting the weights. It demanded all his concentration to keep his eyes off Sherry. Ignoring her was the only thing that seemed to work. "What you wear is none of my concern," he returned blandly.

"I—I don't feel like I'm really exercising unless I wear the helmet," she said next, looking for a smile to crack his tight concentration. She rubbed her hand dry against her shorts. The helmet hadn't been her only idea. She'd strapped a horn and side mirror onto the handlebars of the bike and had later added the sheepskin cover to pad the seat.

Roarke didn't comment.

He looked and sounded so infuriatingly disinterested that Sherry had to clear the tears from her throat before she went on.

"Roarke," she pleaded, "I hate this. I know you have good reason to believe I plotted...what happened in your office." She hesitated long enough for him to consider her words. "I'll be honest with you—that had been exactly my intention in the beginning. But once I got there I realized I couldn't do it."

"For someone who found herself incapable of such a devious action, you succeeded extremely well." He paused and studied her impassively.

"I w-want things to be different. I don't think we'll ever be able to settle anything here at camp, so I'm proposing that we meet in town to talk. I'll be in Ellen's Café tomorrow at six...it's my day off. I hope you'll meet me there."

Roarke wanted things settled, too, but not at the expense of his pride and self-respect.

"Answer me, Roarke. At least have the common courtesy to speak to me." His manner was so distant, so unconcerned that Sherry discovered she had to look away from him or lose her composure entirely.

"There's nothing to say," he returned stiffly.

The prolonged silence in the room was as irritating as fingernails on a blackboard. Sherry couldn't stand it any more than she could tolerate his indifference.

"If that's the way you wish to leave matters, then so be it. I tried; I honestly tried," she said, with such dejection that her voice was hardly audible.

Pointedly, Roarke looked in another direction.

With the dignity of visiting royalty, Sherry tucked her helmet under her arm, lifted her chin an extra notch and left the room. A hot tear slipped down the corner of her cheek. She let it fall, then gave in to the others that came in quick succession. Jeff Roarke was a fool!

"Miss White, Miss White!" Diane ran across the campus to her side and stopped abruptly, cocking her head as she studied her counselor. "You're crying."

Sherry nodded and wiped the moisture from her face with the back of her hand.

"Are you hurt?"

"In a manner of speaking." Diane was much too perceptive to fool. "Someone hurt my feelings, but I'll be all right in a minute."

"Who?" Diane demanded, straightening her shoulders. From the little girl's stance, it looked as though she was prepared to single-handedly take on anyone who had hurt her friend and counselor.

"It doesn't matter who. It's over now, and I'll be fine in a minute." Several afternoons a week, Sherry sat on the lawn and the children from the camp gathered at her feet. As a natural born storyteller, she filled the time with make-believe tales from the classics and history. The children loved it, and Sherry enjoyed spending time with them. "Now what was it you needed?"

Shyly Diane looked away.

Sherry laughed. "No, let me guess. I bet you're after another book. Am I right?"

The youngster nodded. "Can I borrow the last book in the Great Brain series?"

"One great brain to another," Sherry said, forcing the joke.

"Right. Can I?"

Sherry looped her arm around the child's small shoulders. "Sure. This story is really a good one. Tom contacts the Pope... well, never mind, you'll read about it yourself."

They'd gone about halfway across the thick carpet of grass when a piercing scream rent the air. Startled, Sherry turned around and discovered Sally running toward her, blood streaming down her forehead and into her eyes, nearly blinding her.

"Miss White, Miss White," she cried in terror. "I fell! I fell!"

Sherry's stomach curdled at the sight of oozing blood. "Diane," she instructed quickly, "run to the cabin and get me a towel. Hurry, sweetheart."

With her arms flying, Diane took off like a jet from a crowded runway.

"I saw it happen," Gretchen cried, following close on Sally's heels and looking sickly pale. "Sally slipped and hit her head on the side of a desk."

"It's fine, sweetheart," Sherry reassured the injured youngster. She placed her hand on the side of Sally's head and found the gash. Pressing on it gently in an effort to stop the ready flow of blood, she guided the girl toward the infirmary.

"Gretchen, run ahead and let Nurse Butler know we're coming."

"It hurts so bad," Sally wailed.

"I'm sure it does, but you're being exceptionally brave."

Breathless, Diane returned with the towel. Sherry took it and replaced her hand with the absorbent material.

The buzzer rang in the background, indicating that the next class was about to start.

Gretchen and Diane exchanged glances. "I don't want to leave my friend," Gretchen murmured, her voice cracking.

Both Gretchen and Diane were frightened, and sending them away would only increase their dismay and play upon their imaginations, Sherry reasoned.

"You can stay until we're all sure Sally's going to be fine. Now, go do what I said."

Gretchen took off at a full run toward the nurse's office, with Diane in hot pursuit. By the time Sherry reached the infirmary, Kelly Butler, the wife of the younger boys' counselor, had been alerted and was waiting.

"Miss White, I'm scared," Sally said, and sniffled loudly.

"Everything's going to be fine," Sherry assured her miniscientist, standing close to her side.

"Will you stay with me?"

"Of course." Sally was her responsibility, and Sherry wouldn't leave the child when she needed her most—no matter how much blood there was.

"This way." Kelly Butler motioned toward the small examination room.

While maintaining the pressure to the gash, Sherry helped Sally climb onto the table. Gretchen and Diane stood in the doorway, looking on.

"You two will have to stay outside until I'm finished," the nurse informed the two.

Both girls sent pleading glances in Sherry's direction. "Do as she says," Sherry told them. "I'll be out to tell you how Sally is in a few minutes."

Halfway through the examination Sherry started to feel light-headed. Her knees went rubbery, and she reached for a chair and sat down.

"Are you all right?" Kelly asked her.

"I'm fine," she lied.

"Well, it isn't as bad as it looks," the nurse said. She paused to smile at the youngster. "We aren't going to need to take you into Arrow Flats for stitches, but I'll have to cut away your bangs to put on a bandage."

"Can I look at it in a mirror?" The shock and pain had lessened enough for Sally's natural curiosity to take over. "If I don't become a biochemist, then I might decide to be a doctor," Sally explained haughtily.

Sherry's nauseated feeling continued, and forcing a smile, she stood. "I'll go tell Diane and Gretchen that Sally's going to recover before they start planning her funeral."

"Thanks for staying with me, Miss White," Sally said, gripping the hand mirror.

"No problem, kiddo."

"You're going to make a great mom someday."

The way she was feeling caused Sherry to sincerely doubt that. The sight of blood had always bothered her, but never more than now. Taking deep breaths to dispel the sickly sensation, she stood and let herself out of the examination room.

Her two charges were missing. Sherry blinked, but Jeff Roarke, who sat in their place didn't vanish. The light-headed feeling persisted, and she wasn't sure if he was real or a figment of her stressed-out senses.

"How is she?" he asked, coming to his feet.

"Fine." At the moment, Sally was doing better than Sherry. "Head wounds apparently bleed a lot, but it doesn't look like she's going to need stitches."

Roarke nodded somberly. "That's good."

"Where are Diane and Gretchen?"

"I sent them back to class," he told her. "I heard how you took control of the situation."

Sherry bristled. "I suppose you'd prefer to believe that I'd panic when confronted with a bleeding child."

"Of course not," he flared.

Trying desperately to control the attack of dizziness, Sherry reached out and gripped the edge of a table.

"You've got blood on your sweatshirt," Roarke said.

Sherry glanced down and gasped softly as the walls started spinning. She wanted to comment, but before she could the room unexpectedly went black.

Roarke watched in astonishment as Sherry crumpled to the floor. At first he thought she was playing another of her silly games. It would be just like her to pull a crazy stunt like that. Then he noted that her coloring was sickly, almost ashen, and immediately he grew alarmed. This wasn't any trick, she'd actually fainted! He fell to his knees at her side and tossed a desperate look over his shoulder, thinking he should call the nurse. But Kelly was already busy with one patient.

He reached for Sherry's hand and lightly slapped her wrist. He'd seen someone do this in a movie once, but how it was supposed to help, he didn't know. His own heart was hammering out of control. Seeing her helpless this way had the most unusual effect upon him. All week he'd been furious with her, so outraged at her underhandedness that he'd barely been able to look at her and not feel the fire of his anger rekindled. He wasn't particularly proud of his behavior, and he'd chosen to blame Sherry for his ill-temper and ugly moods all week. He'd wanted to forget she was around, and completely cast her from his mind once the summer was over.

Seeing her now, he felt as helpless as a wind-tossed leaf, caught in a swirling updraft of emotion. He loved this woman, and pretending otherwise simply wasn't going to work. She was a schemer, a manipulator... and a joy. She was fresh and alive and unspoiled. The whole camp had been brought to life with her smile. Even though this was her first year as a counselor, she took to it as naturally as someone who had been coming back for several summers. Her mind was active, her wit sharp and she possessed a genuine love for the children. They sensed it and gravitated toward her like bees to a blossoming flower.

She moaned, or he thought she did; the sound was barely audible. Roarke's brows drew together in a heavy frown, and he gently smoothed the hair from her face. He'd never seen anyone faint before and he wasn't sure what to do. He elevated her head slightly and noted evidence of fresh tears. Dealing with Sally's injury hadn't been the source of these. From everything Gretchen and Diane had told him, Sherry had handled the situation without revealing her own alarm. No, he had been the one who'd made her cry by treating her callously in the exercise room.

Roarke's eyes closed as hot daggers of remorse stabbed through him. The urge to kiss her and make up for all the pain he had caused her was more than he could resist. Without giving thought to his actions, he secured his arms beneath her shoulders and raised her. Then tenderly, with only the slightest pressure, he bent to fit his lips over hers.

Chapter Nine

Sherry didn't know what was happening, but the most incredible sensation of warmth and love surrounded her. Unless she was dreaming, Roarke was kissing her. If this was some fantasy, then she never wanted to wake up. It was as though the entire week had never happened and she was once again in Roarke's arms, reveling in the gentleness of his kiss. The potent feelings were far too wonderful to ignore, and she parted her lips, wanting this moment to last forever. She sighed with regret when the warmth left her.

"Sherry?"

Her eyes blinked open and she moaned as piercing sunlight momentarily blinded her. She raised her hand to shield her vision and found Roarke bending over her.

"Roarke?" she asked in a hoarse whisper. "What happened?"

"You fainted."

She surged upright, bracing herself on one elbow. "I did what?"

Roarke's smile was smug. "You fainted."

It took a moment for her to clear her head. "I did?"

"That's what I just said."

"Sally..."

"Is fine," he reassured her. "Do you do this type of thing often?"

Sherry rubbed a hand over her face, although she remained slightly disoriented. "No, it feels weird. I've never been fond of the sight of blood, but I certainly didn't pass out because of it."

"When was the last time you had something to eat?"

Sherry had to think about that. Her appetite had been nil for days. She wasn't in the habit of eating breakfast unless it was something like a quick glass of orange juice and a dry piece of toast. This morning, however, she hadn't bothered with either breakfast or lunch.

"Sherry?" he prompted.

"I don't know when I last ate. Yesterday at dinnertime, I guess." She'd been so miserable that food was the last thing she'd wanted.

Roarke's frown deepened, and his arm tightened around her almost painfully. "Of all the stupid—"

"Oh, stop!" She jerked herself free from his grip and awkwardly rose to her feet. "Go ahead and call me stupid...but why stop with that? You've probably got ten other names you're dying to use on me."

Roarke's mouth thinned, but he didn't rise to the bait. The last thing he'd expected was for her to fight him. This woman astonished him. She was full of surprises and...full of promise. Even when she was semiconscious, she had shyly responded to his kiss. He was embarrassed by the impulse now. Who did he think he was—some kind of legendary lover?

"You're coming with me," he commanded.

"Why? So you can shout at me some more?" she hissed at him like a cat backed into a corner, seeking a means of escape.

"No," he returned softly. "So I can get you something to eat."

"I can take care of myself, thank you very much."

Roarke snickered. "I can tell. Now stop arguing."

Sherry closed her mouth and realized what a fool she was being. For an entire week, she'd wanted to talk to him, spend time alone with him, and now when he'd suggested exactly that, she was making it sound like a capital offense.

Roarke led the way out of the infirmary, and Sherry followed silently behind him. The cooking staff were busy making preparations for the evening meal, and the big kitchen was filled with the hustle and bustle of the day. Roarke approached the cook, who glanced in Sherry's direction and nodded as Roarke said something to him.

Roarke returned to her. "He's going to scramble you some eggs. I suggest you eat them."

"I will," she promised, then watched helplessly as Roarke turned and walked out of the mess hall, leaving her standing alone.

Ellen's Café in Arrow Flats was filled with the week-night dinner crowd. Sherry sat at a table by the window and studied the menu, although she'd read it so many times over the past twenty minutes that she could have recounted it from memory.

"Do you want to order, miss?" the young waitress in the pink uniform asked. "It looks like your friend isn't going to make it."

"No, I think I'll hold off for a few more minutes, if you don't mind."

"No problem. Just give the signal when you're ready."

"I will." Sherry felt terrible. More depressed than she could remember being in months. She'd really hoped tonight with Roarke would make a difference. She'd put such high hopes in the belief that if they could get away from the camp to meet on neutral ground and talk freely, then maybe they could solve the problems between them.

Just then the café door whirled open. Sherry's gaze flew in that direction, her heart rocketing to her throat as Roarke stepped inside. His gaze did a sweeping inspection of the café, and paused when he found Sherry. He sighed and smiled.

To Sherry it seemed that everyone and everything else in the restaurant faded from view.

"Hi," he said, a bit breathlessly, when he joined her. He pulled out the chair across the table from her and sat. "I apologize for being late. Something came up at the last minute, and I couldn't get away."

"Problems at the camp?"

Forcefully, he expelled his breath and nodded. "I don't want to talk about camp tonight. I'm just a lonely college professor looking for a quiet evening."

"I'm just a sweet young thing looking for a college professor seeking a quiet evening."

"I think we've found each other." Roarke's grin relaxed the tight muscles in his face. He'd convinced himself that Sherry had probably left when he didn't show. They both needed this time away from camp. He'd been miserable and so had she.

He was here at last, Sherry mused silently. Roarke was with her, and the dread of the past pain-filled minutes were wiped out with one Jeff Roarke smile.

"Have you ordered?"

Sherry shook her head and lowered her gaze to the memorized menu. "Not yet."

Roarke's eyes dropped, too, as he studied his own. Choosing quickly, he set it beside his plate. "I highly recommend the special."

"Liver and onions? Oh, Roarke, honestly." She laughed because she was so pleased he was there, and because liver and onions sounded exactly like a meal he'd enjoy.

"Doubt me if you will, but when liver hasn't been fried to a crisp, it's good."

Sherry closed her menu and set it aside. "Don't be disappointed, but I think I'll go with the French dip."

Roarke grinned and shook his head. "I never would have believed Miss Sherry White could be so boring."

"Boring!" She nearly choked on a sip of water.

"All right, all right, I'll revise that." Laugh lines formed deep grooves at the corners of his eyes. "I doubt that you'll ever be that. I can see you at a hundred and ten in the middle of a floor learning the latest dance step."

Sherry's hand circled her water glass. "I'll accept that as a compliment." But she didn't want to be on any dance floor if her partner wasn't Jeff Roarke, she added silently.

The amusement drained from his eyes. "What you said yesterday hit home."

Sherry looked up and blinked, uncertain. "About what?"

"That you wanted things to be different between us. I do too, Sherry. If we'd met any place but at camp things would be a hell of a lot easier. I have responsibilities—for that matter, so do you. Camp isn't the place for a relationship—now isn't the time."

Nervously, her fingers toyed with the fork stem. She didn't know what to say. Roarke seemed to be telling her that the best thing for them to do was ignore the attrac-

tion between them, pretend it wasn't there and go on about
their lives as though what they felt toward each other made
no difference.

"I see," she said slowly, her high spirits sinking to the
depths of despair.

"But obviously, that bit of logic isn't going to work,"
Roarke added thoughtfully. "I've tried all week, and look
what happened. I can't ignore you, Sherry, it's too hard on
both of us."

The smile lit up her face. "I can't ignore you, either. As
it turns out, I'm here and you're here."

His eyes held hers. "And there's no place else I'd rather
be. For tonight, at least, we're two people with different
tastes and life-styles who happened to meet in an obscure
café in Arrow Flats, California."

Sherry smiled and nodded eagerly.

The waitress came and took their order, and Sherry and
Roarke talked throughout the meal and long after they'd
finished. They lingered over coffee, neither wanting the
evening to end.

They left the café when *the* Ellen herself appeared from
the kitchen and flipped the sign in the window to Closed.
She paused to stare pointedly at them.

"I have the feeling she wants us to leave," Roarke muttered, looking around and noting for the first time that
they were the only two customers left in the café.

Sherry took one last sip of her coffee and placed her
paper napkin on the tabletop.

Roarke grinned and scooted back his chair to stand, and
Sherry rose and followed him out of the restaurant.

"Where are you parked?" he asked.

"Around the corner."

He reached for her hand, lacing her fingers with his
own. The action produced a soft smile in Sherry. Some-

thing as simple as holding her hand would be out of the question at camp. But tonight it was the most natural thing in the world.

"It's nearly ten," Roarke stated, surprise lifting his husky voice.

It astonished Sherry to realize that they'd sat and talked for more than four hours. Although they hadn't touched until just now, she'd never felt closer to Roarke. When they were at camp it seemed that their differences were magnified a thousandfold by circumstances and duty. Tonight they could be themselves. He'd astonished her. Amused her. Being with Roarke felt amazingly right.

He hesitated in front of the Ford station wagon. The camp logo was printed on the side panel.

Roarke opened the driver's side for her, and Sherry tossed her purse inside. They stood with the car door between them.

"Roarke?" she whispered, curious. "This may sound like a crazy question, but yesterday when I fainted . . . did you kiss me?"

His grin was slightly off center as he answered her with a quick nod of his head. He'd felt like a fool afterward, chagrined by his own actions. He wasn't exactly the model for Prince Charming, waking Sleeping Beauty with a secret kiss.

"I thought you must have," Sherry said softly. She'd felt so warm and secure that she hadn't wanted to wake up. "I was wondering is all," she added, a little flustered when he didn't speak.

Roarke caressed her cheek with his right hand. "Are you worried you'll have to pass out a second time before I do it again?"

She smiled at that. "The thought had crossed my mind."

"No," he said softly, sliding his hand down her face to the gentle slope of her shoulder. "Just move out from behind the car door."

Smiling, she did, deliberately closing it before walking into his arms. Roarke brought her close, breathed in the heady female scent of her and sighed his appreciation. His lips brushed against her temple, savoring the marvelous silken feel of her in his arms and the supreme rightness of holding her close. He kissed her forehead and her cheek, her chin, then closed her eyes with his lips.

His gentleness made Sherry go weak. She slipped her arms up his chest and around his neck, letting his strength absorb her weakness.

Roarke paused to glance with irritation at the streetlight, and suddenly decided he didn't care who saw him with Sherry or any consequences he might suffer as a result. He had to taste her. He kissed her then, deeply, yearning to reveal all the things he couldn't say with words. Urgently, his lips moved over hers with a fierce tenderness, until she moaned and responded, opening her mouth to him with passion and need.

Sherry's husky groan of pleasure throbbed in Roarke's ears and raced through his blood like quicksilver. He kissed her so many times he lost count, and she was weak and clinging to his arms. His own self-restraint was tested to the limit. With every vestige of control he possessed, he broke off the kiss and buried his face in her shoulder. He drew in a long breath and slowly expelled it in an effort to regain his wits and composure. He couldn't believe he was kissing her like this, in the middle of the street, with half the town looking on. Holding her, touching her, had been the only matters of importance.

"I'll follow you back to camp," he said, after a long moment.

Still too befuddled to speak, Sherry nodded.

Roarke dropped his arms and watched reluctantly as she stepped away. It was all he could do not to haul her back into his arms and kiss her senseless. From the first moment that he'd watched her interact with the children, Roarke had known that she was a natural. What he hadn't guessed was that this marvelous woman would hold his heart in the palm of her hand. He couldn't tell Sherry what he felt for her now; to do so would create the very problem he strove to avoid between staff members. Romance and camp were like oil and water, not meant to mix. To leave her doubting was regrettable, but necessary until the time was right. Never, in all the years that he'd been camp director, had Roarke more looked forward to August.

Roarke was busy all the following day. Even if he'd wanted, he wouldn't have been able to talk to Sherry. They passed each other a couple of times but weren't able to exchange anything more than a casual greeting. Now, at the end of another exhausting day, he felt the need to sit with her for a time and talk. For as long as he could, he resisted the temptation. At nine-thirty, Roarke decided no one would question it, if they saw him sitting on her porch talking.

As he neared her cabin, he heard the girls clamoring inside.

"I saw Buttercup," one of the girls cried, the alarm in her voice obvious.

Roarke glanced around, and sure enough, there was his calico, snooping around the cabin, peeking through the window. Naturally, Sherry's girls would be concerned over the feline, since they continued to house the rodent mascot. Every other cabin had welcomed Buttercup, but the cat had made his choice obvious and lingered around

Sherry's, spending far more time there than at all the others combined. Roarke wasn't completely convinced it was solely the allure of Ralph, the hamster, either. Like almost everyone else in camp, the feline wanted to be around Sherry. Roarke watched with interest whenever Fred Spencer voiced his objections. It was obvious to Roarke that the man was jealous of Sherry's popularity, and his resentment shone through at each staff meeting.

"I saw him, too!" The commotion inside the cabin continued.

Roarke climbed the three steps that led to the front door and crouched down to pick up his cat.

"Now," Sherry's excited voice came at him from inside the cabin.

Just as he'd squatted down the front door flew open, and he looked up to find Sherry standing directly in front of him, pointing a Thompson submachine gun directly at his chest.

Before he could shout a warning, a piercing blast of water hit him square in the chest.

Chapter Ten

The blast of water was powerful enough to knock Roarke off balance. Crouched as he was, the force, coupled with the shock of Sherry aiming a submachine gun at him, hurled him backward.

"Roarke," Sherry screamed and slapped her hand over her mouth, smothering her horror, which soon developed into an out-and-out laugh.

Buttercup meowed loudly and scrambled from Roarke's grip, darting off into the night.

"Who the hell do you think you are?" Roarke yelled. "Rambo?" With as much dignity as he could muster, he stood and brushed the grit from his buttocks and hands.

"Mr. Roarke said the H-word." Righteously, Gretchen turned and whispered to the others.

Six small heads bobbed up and down in unison. Unlike Sherry, they recognized that this wasn't the time to show their amusement. Mr. Roarke didn't seem to find the incident the least bit humorous.

"I'm going to say a whole lot more than the H-word if you don't put that gun away," he shouted, his features tight and impatient.

Doing her utmost to keep from smiling, Sherry lowered her weapon, pointing the extended barrel toward the hardwood floor. "I apologize, Roarke, I wasn't aiming for you. I thought Buttercup was alone."

"That cat happens to be the camp pet," he yelled. He paused and inhaled a steadying breath before continuing. "Perhaps it would be best if we spoke privately, Miss White. Girls, if you'd kindly excuse us a moment."

"Oh, sure, go ahead," Gretchen answered for the group, and the others nodded in agreement.

"Sure," Jill and Jan added.

"Feel free," Sally inserted.

"Why not?" Diane wanted to know.

The amusement drained from Sherry's eyes. So much for the new wonderful understanding between them and the evening they'd spent together in town. Roarke knew how much she hated it when he sarcastically called her Miss White. No one did it quite the way he did, saying her name with all the coldness of arctic snow. Snow White. That's what the girls liked to call her when she wasn't around, although they didn't think she knew it.

Sherry stepped onto the porch and Roarke closed the door. "I do apologize, Roarke." Maybe if she said it enough times he'd believe her.

"I sincerely doubt that," he grumbled, swatting the moisture from his shirt. "Good grief, woman, don't you ever do anything like anyone else?"

"I was protecting Ralph," she cried, growing agitated. "What was I supposed to do? Invite Buttercup in for lunch and break seven little girls' hearts?"

"I certainly don't expect you to drown him."

"Fiddlesticks!" she returned heatedly, staring him down. "You're just mad because I got you wet. Believe me, it was unintentional. If I'd known you were going to be on the other side of the door, do you honestly think I would have pulled the trigger?"

"You'll do anything for a laugh," he countered.

Sherry was so furious, she could barely speak. "I might as well have, you're a wet blanket anyway." Following that announcement, she marched into the cabin and slammed the door.

Regret came instantly. What was she doing? Sherry wailed inwardly. She'd behaved like a child when she so much wanted to be a woman. But Roarke always assumed the worst of her, and his lack of trust was what hurt most.

Roarke had half a mind to follow her. He opened his mouth to demand that she come back out or he'd have her job, but the anger drained from him, leaving him flustered and impatient. For a full minute he didn't move. Finally he wiped his hand across his face, shrugged and headed back to his quarters, defeated and discouraged.

That night, Roarke lay in bed thinking. Sherry possessed more spirit than any woman he'd ever known. He would have loved to get a picture of the expression on her face once she realized she'd blasted him with that crazy weapon. But instead of laughing as they should have, the episode had ended in a shouting match. It seemed he did everything wrong with this woman. Maybe if he hadn't kept his nose buried in a book most of his life he'd know more about dealing with the opposite sex. Fiona was so much like him that they'd drifted together for no other reason than that they shared several interests. As he lay in bed, Roarke wasn't sure he could even remember what Fiona looked like.

He'd never been a ladies' man, although he wasn't so naive as to not realize that the opposite sex found him attractive. The scars of his youth went deep. The bookworm, four-eyes and all the other names he'd been taunted with echoed in the farthest corners of his mind. As an adult he'd avoided women, certain that they would find his intelligence and his dedication to the child genius a dead bore. He was thirty, but when it came to this unknown, unsettling realm of romance, he seemed to have all the social grace of a sixteen-year-old.

"Miss White," Pamela called into the dark silence.

"Yes?" Sherry sat upright and glanced at the bedside clock. Although it was well past midnight, she hadn't been able to sleep. "Is something wrong, honey?"

"No."

The direction of the small voice told Sherry that Pamela's head hung low. "Come here, and we can talk without waking the others." Sherry patted the flat space beside her and pulled back the covers so Pam could join her in bed.

The little girl found her way in the dark and climbed onto the bed. Sherry sat upright and leaned against the thick pillows, wrapping her arm around the nine-year-old's shoulders.

"It's Ralph's fault, isn't it?" Pamela said in a tiny, indistinct voice.

"What is?"

"That Mr. Roarke yelled at you."

"Honey," Sherry said with a sigh, "how can you possibly think that? I squirted Mr. Roarke with a submachine gun. He had every right to be upset."

"But you wouldn't have shot him if it hadn't been for Ralph. And then he got mad, and it's all my fault because

I smuggled Ralph on the airplane without anyone knowing."

"Mr. Roarke had his feathers ruffled is all. There isn't anything to worry about."

Pamela raised her head and blinked. "Will he send you away?"

Knowing that Roarke could still find out that she'd deceived him on the application form didn't lend her confidence. "I don't think so, and if he does it'd be for something a lot more serious than getting him wet."

Pamela shook her head. "My mom and dad shout at each other the way you and Mr. Roarke do."

"We don't mean to raise our voices," Sherry said, feeling depressed. "It just comes out that way. Things will be better tomorrow." Although she tried to give them confidence, Sherry's words fell decidedly flat.

Throughout the staff meeting the following morning Sherry remained withdrawn and quiet. When Roarke didn't seek her out when the session was dismissed, she returned to her cabin. The girls, too, were quiet, regarding her with anxious stares.

"Well?" Gretchen finally demanded.

"Well, what?" Sherry asked, pulling a sweatshirt over her head, then freeing her hair from the constricting collar. When she finished, she turned to find all seven of the girls studying her.

"How did things go with Mr. Roarke?"

"Is he still angry?"

"Did he yell at you again?"

Sherry raised her hands to stop them. "Everything went fine."

"Fine?" Seven thin voices echoed hers.

"All right, it went great," Sherry sputtered. "Okay, let's move it—it's breakfast time."

A chorus of anxious cries followed her announcement as the girls scrambled for their sweaters, books and assorted necessities.

For most of the day Sherry stayed to herself, wanting to avoid another confrontation with Roarke. However, by late afternoon, she felt as if she was suffering from claustrophobia, avoiding contact with the outside world, ignoring the friends she'd made this summer. There had to be a better way!

Most of the classes had been dismissed, and Sherry sat on the porch steps of her cabin, watching the children chasing one another about, laughing and joking. The sound of their amusement was sweet music to her ears. It hadn't been so long ago that she'd wondered about these minigeniuses, and she was pleased to discover they were learning to be children and have fun. Several of the youngsters were playing games she'd taught them.

A breathless Gretchen soon joined Sherry, sitting on the step below hers. As was often the case when Sherry was within view of the children, she was soon joined by a handful of others.

"Will you tell me the story about how the star got inside the apple again?" Gretchen asked. "I tried to tell Gloria, but I forgot part of it."

"Sure," Sherry said with a grin and proceeded to do just that. Someone supplied her with an apple and a knife, and she took the fruit and cut it crosswise at the end of the story, holding it up to prove to the growing crowd of children that there was indeed a star in every apple.

Fred Spencer approached as she was speaking, pursing his lips in open disapproval. Sherry did her best to ignore him. She didn't understand what Fred had against her, but she was weary of the undercurrents of animosity she felt whenever he was near.

"Shouldn't these children be elsewhere?" he asked, his voice tight and slightly demanding.

Sherry stood and met the glaring dislike in the other man's eyes. "Okay, children, it's time to return to your cabins."

The small group let out a chorus of groans, loudly voicing their protest. Reluctantly, they left Sherry's side, dragging their feet.

"Oh, Miss White," Gretchen murmured. "I forgot to give you this." She withdrew an envelope from her pocket. The camp logo was stamped on the outside. "Mr. Roarke asked me to give this to you. I'm sorry I forgot."

"No problem, sweetheart." Sherry reached for the letter, her heart clamoring. Although she was dying to read what Roarke had written, Sherry held off, staring at her name, neatly centered on the outside of the business-size envelope. Fleetingly, she wondered if Roarke had decided to fire her. Then she realized that he wouldn't have asked Gretchen to deliver the notice; he had more honor than that.

With trembling fingers and a pounding heart, she tore off the end of the envelope, blew inside to open it and withdrew a single sheet. Carefully unfolding it, she read the neatly typed sentence in the middle of the page: Midnight at Clear Lake. Jeff Roarke.

Sherry read the four-word message over and over again. Midnight at the lake? It didn't make sense. Was he proposing that she meet him there? The two of them, alone? Surely there was some other hidden meaning that she was missing. After the incident with Buttercup, he had her so flustered she couldn't think straight.

During the evening, Sherry flirted with the idea of ignoring the note entirely, but as the sun set and dusk crept across the campgrounds, bathing the lush property in golden hues, she knew in her heart that no matter what happened she'd be at the lake as Jeff Roarke had requested.

At five minutes to midnight, she checked her seven charges to be sure they were sleeping and woke Ginny long enough to tell her she was leaving. As silently as possible, Sherry slipped from the cabin. The moon was three-quarters full and cast a silken glow of light on the pathway that led to the lake's edge.

Hugging her arms, Sherry made her way along the well-defined walkway. Roarke's message hadn't been specific about where she was to meet him, although she'd read the note a hundred times. She pulled the letter from the hip pocket of her jeans and read the four words again.

"Sherry."

Roarke's voice startled her. Alarmed, Sherry slapped a hand over her heart.

"Sorry, I didn't mean to frighten you."

"That's all right," she said, quick to reassure him. "I should have been listening for you." He looked so tall and handsome in the moonlight, and her heart quickened at the sight of him. Loving him felt so right. A thousand times over the past few days she'd had doubts about caring so much for Roarke, but not now. Not tonight.

"Shall we sit down?"

"It's a beautiful night, isn't it?" Sherry asked as she lowered herself onto the sandy beach. They used an old log to lean against and paused to gaze into the heavens. The lake lapped lazily a few yards from their feet, and a fresh cool breeze carried with it the sweet, distinctive scent of summer. The moment was serene, unchallenged by the churning problems that existed between them.

"It's a lovely evening," he answered after a moment. He drew his knees up, crossed his legs and sighed expres-

sively. "I'm pleased you did this, Sherry. I felt badly about
the episode with the squirt gun."

"You're pleased I did this?" she returned. "What do
you mean?"

"The note."

"What note? I didn't send you any note, but I did receive yours."

"Mine!" He turned then to study her, his gaze wide and
challenging.

"I have it right here." Agilely, she raised her hips and
slipped the paper from her pocket. It had been folded several times over, and her fingers fumbled with impatience
as she opened it to hand to him.

Roarke's gaze quickly scanned the few words. "I didn't
write this."

"Of course you did." He couldn't deny it now. The sta-
tionery and envelope were both stamped with the Camp
Gitche Gumee logo.

"Sherry, I'm telling you I didn't write that note, but I
did receive yours."

"And I'm telling you I didn't send you one."

"Then who did?"

She shrugged and gestured with her hand. She had a fair
idea who was responsible. Her wizards! All seven of them!
They'd plotted this romantic rendezvous down to the last
detail, and both Roarke and Sherry had been gullible
enough to fall for it. It would have angered Sherry, but for
the realization that Roarke had wanted these few stolen
moments badly enough to believe even the most improb-
able circumstances.

Roarke cleared his throat. He could feel Sherry's
mounting agitation and sought a way to reassure her. He
wasn't so naive as not to recognize that her girls must be
responsible for this arrangement. Hell, he didn't care. She

was sitting at his side in the moonlight, and it felt so good to have her with him that he didn't want anything to ruin it.

"It seems to me," he said slowly, measuring his words, "that this is Longfellow's doing."

"Longfellow?" Sherry repeated. Then she relaxed, a smile growing until she felt the relief and amusement surge up within her. "Yes, it must be him."

"Camp Gitche Gumee's own personal ghost—Longfellow," Roarke repeated softly. He paused, lifted his arm and cupped her shoulder, bringing her closer into his embrace.

Sherry let her head rest against the solid strength of his shoulder. Briefly she closed her eyes to the swelling tide of emotion that enveloped her. Roarke beside her, so close she could smell his after-shave and the manly scent that was his alone. He was even closer in spirit, so that it was almost as if the words to communicate were completely unnecessary.

Silence reigned for the moment, a refreshing reprieve to the anger that had so often unexpectedly erupted between them. This was a rare time, and Sherry doubted that either would have allowed anyone or anything to destroy it.

"We do seem to find ways to clash, don't we?" Sherry said, after a long moment. They'd made a point of not talking about life at camp when they'd had dinner, but tonight it was necessary. "Roarke, I want you to know I've never intentionally gone out of my way to irritate you."

"I had to believe that," he said softly, gently rifling his fingers through her soft dark hair. "Otherwise I would have gone a little crazy. But maybe I did anyway," he added as an afterthought.

"It just seems that everything I do—is wrong."

"Not wrong," he corrected, his voice raised slightly. "Just different. Some of your ideas have been excellent, but a few of the other counselors . . ."

"Fred Spencer." Roarke didn't need to mention names for her to recognize her most outspoken opponent. Almost from the day of her arrival, Fred had criticized her efforts with the children and challenged her ideas.

"Yes, Fred," Roarke admitted.

"Why?"

"He's been with the camp for as long as we've been operating, dedicating his summers to the children. It's been difficult for him to accept your popularity. The kids love you."

"But I don't want to compete with him."

"He'll learn that soon enough. You've shown admirable restraint, Sherry. The others admire you for the way you've dealt with Fred." He turned his head just enough so that his lips grazed her temple as he spoke. "The others nothing; *I've* admired you."

"Oh, Roarke."

His arm around her tightened, and Sherry held her breath. The magic was potent, so very potent. His breath fanned her cheek, searing her flushed skin. Without being aware that she was rotating her head toward him, Sherry turned, silently seeking his kiss.

Roarke's hand touched her chin and tipped her face toward him. Sherry stared up at him, hardly able to believe what she saw in his eyes and felt in her heart. His gaze was full of warmth and tenderness and he was smiling with such sweet understanding. It seemed that Roarke was telling her with his eyes how important she was to him, how much he enjoyed her wit, her creativity. Her.

Slowly he bent his head to her. Sherry slid her hands up his shoulders and tilted her head to meet him halfway. He groaned her name, and his lips came down to caress hers in a long, undemanding, tender kiss that robbed her lungs of breath.

The kiss deepened as Roarke sensually shaped and molded her lips to his. Sherry gave herself over to him, holding back nothing. He kissed her again and again, unable to get enough of the delicious taste of her. She was honey and wine. Unbelievably sweet. Sunshine and love. He kissed her again, then lifted his head to tenderly cup her face between his large hands and gaze into her melting brown eyes.

"Roarke?" she said his name, not knowing herself what she would ask. It was in her to beg him not to stop for fear that something would pull them apart as it had so often in the past.

"You're so sweet," he whispered, unable to look away. His mouth unerringly found hers, the kiss lingering, slow and compelling so that by the time he raised his head Sherry was swimming in a sea of sensual awareness.

"Roarke, why do we argue?" Her hands roamed through his hair, luxuriating in the thick feel of it between her fingers. "I hate it when we do."

"Me, too, love. Me, too." His tongue flickered over the seam of her lips, teasing them at first, then urging them apart. And when she did open her mouth, his tongue plunged inside to intimately explore the silken hollow with such thoroughness that Sherry was left weak with desire, clinging to him as the only secure thing in a world that had unexpectedly gone spinning off course.

"Sherry, love," he whispered, and inhaled deeply. "We have to stop."

"I know," she answered and nodded.

But neither loosened the embrace. Neither was willing to forsake the moment or relinquish this special closeness growing between them.

Roarke rubbed his moist mouth sensuously against hers. Back and forth, until Sherry thought she would faint with wanting him. When she could tolerate it no longer, she parted her lips and once again they were tossed into the roiling sea of passion.

Without warning, Roarke stopped.

Kissed into senselessness, Sherry could do nothing to protest. Breathing had taken on an extraordinary effort, and she pressed her forehead to his chest while she gathered her composure.

"Roarke," she whispered.

"In a minute."

She raised her gaze enough to view the naked turmoil that played so vividly across his contorted features.

"I'm sorry," she told him. "So sorry for what happened with Lynn and Peter that day. Sorry for so many things. I can't have you believing that I'd use you like that. I couldn't . . . I just couldn't."

His smile was so gentle that Sherry felt stinging tears gather in her eyes.

"I know," he said softly. "That's in the past and best forgotten."

"But, Roarke, I . . ."

He placed his index finger across her lips, stopping her. "Whatever it is doesn't matter."

Sherry's wide-eyed gaze studied him. She dreaded the moment he learned the whole truth about her. "But I want to be honest."

"You can't lie," he said as his hands lovingly caressed the sides of her face. "I've noticed that about you."

"But I have—"

"It doesn't matter now, Sherry. Not now." Unable to resist her a moment longer, he bent low and thoroughly kissed her again.

Any argument, any desire for Sherry to tell him about the falsified references was tossed aside as unimportant and inconsequential. Within a few weeks the camp session would be over, and if he hadn't discovered the truth by then, she would simply trust that he never would. Later, much later, she'd tell him, and they could laugh about it, her deception a source of amusement.

Roarke stood, offering Sherry his hand to help her to her feet. She took it and pulled herself up, then paused momentarily to brush the sand from her backside and look out over the calm lake. This summer with Roarke would always be remembered as special, but she didn't want it to end. The weeks had flown past, and she couldn't imagine ever being without him now.

With a sigh of regret to be leaving the tranquil scene, Roarke draped his arm over her shoulder and guided her back to the main campgrounds.

"My appreciation to Longfellow," he whispered outside her cabin door.

They shared a secret smile, and with unspoken agreement resisted the urge to kiss good-night.

"I'll tell the girls—Longfellow—you said so," she murmured.

Roarke continued to hold her hand. "Good night, Sherry."

"Good night, Roarke." Reluctantly he released her fingers, moved back and turned away.

"Roarke?" she called, anxiously rising onto her tiptoes.

He turned around. "Yes?"

She stared at him, uncertain; her feet returned to the porch. It was in her mind to ask his forgiveness for everything she'd done that had been so zany and caused him such grief. She yearned to confess everything, clean the slate, but anxiety stopped her. She was afraid that a confession now would ruin everything. She could think of only one thing to say. "Friends?"

"Yes," he answered and nodded for emphasis. Much more than friends, he added silently. Much more.

Things changed after that night. Roarke changed. Sherry changed. Camp Gitche Gumee changed.

It seemed to Sherry that Roarke had relaxed and lowered his guard. Gone was the stiff, unbending camp director. Gone was the tension that stretched between them so taut that Sherry had sometimes felt ill with it. Gone were the days when she'd felt on edge every time they met. Now she eagerly anticipated each meeting.

Roarke spent less time in his office and was often seen talking to the children. The sound of his amusement could frequently be heard drifting across the campgrounds. He joked and smiled, and every once in a while, he shared secret glances with Sherry. These rare moments had the most curious effect upon her. Where she'd always been strong, now she felt weak, yet her weakness was her strength. She'd argued with Roarke, battled for changes, and now she was utterly content. The ideas she'd fought so long and hard to instill at the camp came naturally with her hardly saying a word.

The late afternoons became a special time for Roarke and Sherry with the camp kids. All ages would gather around the couple, and Sherry would lead an impromptu songfest, teaching them songs she'd learned as a youngster at camp. Some were silly songs, while others were more serious, but all were fun, and more than anything, Sherry wanted the children of Camp Gitche Gumee to have fun.

Soon the other counselors and staff members joined Sherry and Roarke on the front lawn, and music became a scheduled event of the day, with two other musically in-clined counselors taking turns leading the songs. Within a week, as if by magic, two guitars appeared, and Sherry played one and Lynn the other, accompanying the singers.

Someone suggested a bonfire by the lake, and the entire camp roasted marshmallows as the sky filled with twin-kling stars.

When they'd finished the first such event in the history of the camp, Gretchen requested that Sherry tell everyone about Longfellow, and after a tense moment, Sherry stepped forward and kept the group spellbound with her make-believe tales.

To her surprise, Roarke added his own comical version of a trick the friendly spook had once played on him when he'd first arrived at the camp. Even Fred Spencer had been amused, and Sherry had caught him chuckling.

The night was such a success that Sherry was too ex-cited to sleep. Her charges were worn-out from the long week and slept peacefully, curled up in their cots. Sherry sat on top of her bed and tried to read, but her thoughts kept wandering to Roarke and how much had changed between them and how much better it was to be with him than any man she'd ever known.

The pebble against her window caught her attention.

"Sherry?" Her name came on a husky whisper.

Stumbling to her feet, she pushed up the window and leaned out. "Who's there?"

"How many other men do you have pounding on your window?"

"Roarke?" Her eyes searched the night for him, but saw nothing. "I know you're out there."

"Right again," he said, and stepped forward, his hands hidden behind his back.

Sherry sighed her pleasure, propped her elbows against the windowsill and cupped her face with her hands. "What are you doing here?"

He ignored the question. "Did you enjoy tonight?"

Sherry nodded eagerly. "It was wonderful." *He* was wonderful!

"Couldn't you sleep?" he asked, then added, "I saw your light on."

"No, I guess I'm too keyed up. What about you?"

"Too happy."

Sherry studied the curious way he stood, with his hands behind him. "What have you got?"

"What makes you think I have anything?"

"Roarke, honestly."

"All right, all right." He swept his arm around and presented her with a small bouquet of wildflowers.

The gift was so unexpected and so special that Sherry was speechless. For the first time in years she struggled to find the words. She yearned to let him know how pleased she was with his gift.

"Oh, Roarke, thank you," she said after a lengthy moment. "I'm stunned." She cupped the flowers in her hand and brought them to her face to savor the sweet scent.

"I couldn't find any better way to let you know I think you're marvelous."

Their eyes held each other's. "I think you're marvelous, too," she told him.

He wanted to kiss her so much it frightened him—more than the night they'd sat by the lake. More than the first time in his office. But he couldn't. She knew it. He knew it. Yet that didn't make refusing her easy.

"Well, I guess I'd better get back."

Sherry's gaze dropped to the bouquet. "Thank you, Roarke," she said again, with tears in her throat. "For everything."

"No." His eyes grew dark and serious. "It's me who should be thanking you."

He'd been gone a full five minutes before Sherry closed the window. She slumped onto the end of her bed and released a sigh. In her most farfetched dreams, she hadn't believed Jeff Roarke could be so wonderfully romantic. Now she prayed nothing would happen to ruin this bliss.

Chapter Eleven

Sleepy and Grumpy are at it again," Wendy told Sherry early the next morning. "Diane doesn't want to wake up and Gretchen's complaining that she didn't sleep a wink on that lumpy mattress."

With only a week left of camp, the girls seemed all the more prone to complaints and minor disagreements. Sherry and the other counselors had endured more confusion these past seven days than at any other time in the two-month-long session of Camp Gitche Gumee.

"Say, where'd you get the flowers?" Jan and Jill blocked the doorway into Sherry's room. Jill had long since lost her tooth, making it almost impossible to tell one twin from the other.

Sherry's gaze moved from Jan and Jill to the bouquet of wildflowers Roarke had given her. They had withered long before, but she couldn't bear to part with them. Every time she looked at his gift she went all weak inside with the memory of the night he'd stood outside her window. The warm, caressing look in his eyes had remained with her all week. She'd never dreamed Jeff Roarke could be so romantic. Pulling herself up straight, Sherry diverted her attention from the wilted wildflowers and thoughts of Roarke. If she lingered any longer, they'd all be late to the mess hall.

Taking charge, Sherry stepped out of her room and soundly clapped her hands twice. "All right, Sleeping Beauty, out of bed."

"She must mean me," Gretchen announced with a wide yawn and tossed aside her covers.

"I believe Miss White was referring to Diane," Wendy said, wrinkling up her nose in a mocking gesture of superiority.

"I was speaking to whoever was still in bed," Sherry said hurriedly, hoping to forestall an argument before it escalated into a shouting match.

"See," Gretchen muttered and stuck out her tongue at Wendy, who immediately responded in kind.

"Girls, please, you're acting like a bunch of ten-year-olds!" It wasn't until after the words had slipped from her mouth that Sherry realized her wizards *were* ten-year-olds! Like Roarke, she'd fallen into the trap of thinking of them as pint-size adults. When she first arrived at camp, she'd been critical of Roarke and the others for their attitudes toward the children. She realized now that she'd been wrong to be so judgmental. The participants of Camp Gitche Gumee weren't normal children. Nor were they little adults, of course, but something special in between.

Moving at a snail's pace that drove Sherry near the brink of losing her control, the girls dressed, collected their books and headed in an orderly fashion for the dining hall. Sherry sat at the head of the table, and the girls followed obediently into their assigned seats.

"I hate mush," Gretchen said, glaring down at the serving bowl that steamed with a large portion of the cooked cereal.

"It's good for you," Sally, the young scientist, inserted.

Diane nodded knowingly. "I read this book about how healthy fiber is in the diet."

Gretchen looked around at the faces staring at her and sighed. "All right, all right. Don't make a big deal over it—I'll eat the mush. But it'll taste like glue, and I'll probably end up at Ms. Butler's office having my stomach pumped."

When Roarke approached the front of the mess hall and the podium, the excited chatter quickly fizzled to a low murmur and then to a hush.

Sherry's gaze rested on the tall director, and even now, after all these weeks, her heart fluttered at the virile sight he made. She honestly loved this man. If anyone had told her the first week after her arrival at camp how she'd feel about Jeff Roarke by the end of the summer, she would have laughed in his face. She recalled the way Roarke had irritated her and his dictatorial ways—but she hadn't known him then, hadn't come to appreciate his quiet strength and subtle wit. She hadn't sat under the stars with him or experienced the thrill of his kisses.

Now, in less than a week, camp would be dismissed and she'd be forced to return to Seattle. Already her mind had devised ways to stay close to Roarke in the next months. A deep inner voice urged her to let him speak first. Most of the times they'd clashed had been when Sherry had proceeded with some brilliant scheme without discussing it with Roarke first. No—as difficult as it would be, she'd wait for him to make the first move. But by heaven that was going to be hard.

When Roarke's announcements for the day were completed, the children were dismissed. With an eager cry, they crowded out of the mess hall door to their first classes.

Sherry remained behind to linger over coffee. Soon Roarke and Lynn joined her.

"Morning," Sherry greeted them both, but her gaze lingered on Roarke. Their eyes met in age-old communication, and all her doubts flew out the window and evaporated into the warm morning air. No man could look at her the way he did and not care. Her tongue felt as if it was stuck to the roof of her mouth and her insides twisted with the potency of his charm.

"The natives are restless," Lynn groaned, cupping her coffee mug with both hands.

"Yes, I noticed that," Roarke commented, but his gaze continued to hold Sherry's. With some effort he pulled his eyes away. Disguising his love for her had become nearly impossible. Another week and he would have the freedom to tell her how much he loved her and to speak of the future, but for now he must bide his time. However, now that camp was drawing to a close, he found that his pulse raced like a locomotive speeding out of control whenever he was around her. His hands felt sweaty, his mouth dry. He'd discovered the woman with whom he could spend the rest of his life and he felt as callow as a boy on his first date.

"The kids need something to keep their minds off the last days of camp," Sherry offered.

"I agree," Lynn added. "I thought your suggestion about a hike to study wildflowers was a good one, Sherry. Whatever became of that?"

Fred Spencer had nixed that plan at a time when Roarke might have approved the idea, had he not been so upset with Sherry. She couldn't remember what had been the problem: Longfellow or their first kiss. Probably both. It seemed she'd continually been in hot water with Roarke in the beginning. How things had changed!

"Now that I think about an organized hike, it sounds like something we might want to investigate," Roarke commented, after mulling over the idea for a couple of minutes.

Sherry paused, uncertain, remembering Fred. "What about . . . you know who?"

"After a couple more days like this one, Fred Spencer will be more than happy to have you take his group for an afternoon."

"We could scout out the area this morning," Lynn suggested, looking to Sherry for confirmation.

"Sure," Sherry returned enthusiastically. She'd had a passion for wildflowers from the time she was ten and camped at Paradise on Washington state's Mount Rainier with her father; hiking together, they'd stumbled upon a field of blazing yellow and white flowers.

"Then you have my blessing," Roarke told the two women, grinning. "Let me know what you find and we'll go from there."

When Sherry and Lynn returned to camp after their successful exploratory hike of the area surrounding the camp and the lake, there was barely time to wash before lunch. Although Sherry was eager to discuss what she'd found with Roarke, she was forced into joining her girls in the mess hall first.

The wizards chattered incessantly, arguing over a paper napkin and a broken shoelace. Wendy reminded everyone that Ken-Richie was still in the hands of a no-good, lily-livered thief and she wasn't leaving camp until he was returned.

The meal couldn't be over soon enough to suit Sherry. The minute the campers were excused, she eagerly crossed the yard to Roarke's office. He hadn't made an appearance at the meal, which was unusual, but it happened often enough not to alarm Sherry.

When she reached his office, she noted that he was alone and knocked politely.

"Come in." His voice was crisp and businesslike.

He looked up from his desk when Sherry walked into the room, but revealed no emotion.

"Is this a bad time?" she asked, hesitant. She could hardly remember the last time he'd spoken to her in that wry tone. Nor had he smiled, and that puzzled her. Her instincts told her something was wrong. His eyes narrowed when he looked at her, and Sherry swallowed her concern. "Do you want me to come back later?"

"No." He shook his head for emphasis. "What did you find?"

"We discovered the most beautiful flowers," she said, warming to the subject closest to her heart. "Oh, Roarke, the trail is perfect. It shouldn't take any more than an hour for the round trip, and I can show the kids several different types of wildflowers. There are probably hundreds more, but those few were the ones I could identify readily. The kids are going to love this."

Her eyes were fairly sparkling with enthusiasm, Roarke noted. Seeing her as she was at this moment made it almost impossible to be angry. His stomach churned, and he looked away, hardly able to bear the sight of her. The phone call had caught him off guard. He'd had most of the morning to come to grips with himself and had failed. Something had to be done, but he wasn't sure what.

"When do you think we could start the first hikes? I mean if you think we should, that is." He was so distant—so strange. Sherry didn't know how she should react. When she first entered the office she'd thought he was irritated with her for something, but now she realized it was more than anger. He seemed distressed, and Sherry hadn't a clue if the matter concerned her or some camp issue. Several times over the past couple of months, she'd been an eyewitness to the heavy pressures placed upon Roarke. He did a marvelous job of managing Camp Gitche Gumee and had gained her unfailing loyalty and admiration.

"Roarke?"

"Hmm?" His gaze left the scene outside his window and reluctantly returned to her.

"Is something wrong?"

"Nothing," he lied smoothly, straightening his shoulders. "Nothing at all. Now regarding the hike, let's give it a trial run. Take your girls out this afternoon and we'll see how things go. Then tomorrow morning you can give a report to the other counselors."

Sherry clasped her hands together, too excited to question him further. "Thank you, Roarke, you won't regret this."

His stoic look was all the response he gave her.

As Sherry knew they would, the girls, carrying backpacks, grumbled all the way from the camp to the other side of the small lake. The pathway was well-defined, and they walked single file along the narrow dirt passage.

"Just how long is this going to take?"

"My feet hurt."

"No one said the Presidential Commission on Physical Fitness applied at Camp Gitche Gumee."

Listening to their complaints brought a smile to Sherry's features. "Honestly," she said with a short laugh, "you guys make it sound like we're going to climb Mount Everest."

"This is more like K-2."

"K-what?" Jan and Jill wanted to know.

"That's the highest peak in the Himalayas," Sally announced with a prim look. In response to a blank stare from a couple of the others, she added, "You know? The mountain system of south-central Asia that extends fifteen hundred miles through Kashmir, northern India, southern Tibet, Nepal, Sikkim and Bhutan."

"I remember reading about those," Diane added.

Gretchen paused and wiped her hot, perspiring face with the back of her hand. "You read about everything," she told her friend.

"Well, that's better than complaining about everything."

"Girls, please," Sherry said, hoping to keep the peace. "This is supposed to be fun."

"Do we get to eat anything?" Jan muttered.

"We're starved," Jill added.

The others agreed in a loud plea until Sherry reminded them that they'd left the mess hall only half an hour before.

"But don't worry," she said, "it's against camp policy to leave the grounds without chocolate chips." Sherry did her best to hide a smile.

Pamela laughed, and the others quickly joined in.

For all their bickering, Sherry's wizards were doing well—and even enjoying themselves. With so much time spent in the classroom in academic ventures, there had been little planned exercise for the girls.

"We'll take a break in a little bit," Sherry promised.

"It's a good thing," Gretchen muttered despairingly.

"Really," Sally added.

"Don't listen to them, Miss White," Pamela piped in, then lowered her voice to a thin whisper. "They're wimps."

"Hey! Look who's calling a wimp a wimp!"

In mute consternation, Sherry raised her arms and silenced her young charges. Before matters got out of hand, she found a fallen log and instructed them to sit.

Grumbling, the girls complied.

"Snack time," Sherry told them, gathering her composure. She slipped the bulky backpack from her tired shoulders. "This is a special treat, developed after twenty years of serious research."

"What is it?" Sally wanted to know, immediately interested in anything that had to do with research.

Already Gretchen was frowning with practiced disapproval.

Sherry ignored their questions and pulled a full jar of peanut butter from inside her pack. She screwed off the lid and reached for a plastic knife. "Does everyone have clean hands?"

Seven pairs of eyes scanned seven pairs of hands. This was followed by eager nods.

"Okay," Sherry told them next, "stick out an index finger."

Silently, they complied and shared curious glances as Sherry proceeded down the neat row of girls, spreading peanut butter on seven extended index fingers. A loud chorus of questions followed.

"Yuk. What's it for?"

"Hey, what are we suppose to do with this?"

"Can I lick it off yet?"

Replacing the peanut butter in her knapsack, Sherry took out a large bag of semisweet chocolate chips.

"What are you going to do with that?"

"Is it true what you said about not leaving camp without chocolate chips?"

"Scout's honor!" Dramatically, Sherry crossed her heart with her right hand, then tore open the bag of chocolate pieces, holding it open for the girls. "Okay, dip your finger inside, coat it with chips and enjoy."

Gretchen was the first to stick her finger in her mouth. "Hey, this isn't bad."

"It's delicious, I promise," Sherry told her wizards as she proceeded from one girl to the next.

"It didn't really take twenty years of research for this, did it?" Sally asked, cocking her head at an angle to study her counselor.

Sherry grinned. "Well, I was about twenty when I perfected the technique." She swirled her finger in the air, then claimed it was all in the wrist movement.

The girls giggled, and the sound of their amusement drifted through the tall redwoods that dominated the forest. Sherry found a rock and sat down in front of her wizards, bringing her knees up and crossing her ankles.

"When I was about your age," she began, "my dad and I went for a hike much like we're doing today. And like you, I complained and wanted to know how much farther I was going to have to walk and how long it would be before I could have something to eat and where the closest rest room was."

The girls continued licking the chocolate and peanut butter off their fingers, but their gazes centered on Sherry.

"When we'd been gone about an hour, I was convinced my dad was never going back to the car. He kept telling me there was something he wanted me to see."

"Can you tell us what it was?"

"Did you ever find it?"

"Yes, to both questions," Sherry said, coming to her feet. "In fact, I want to show you girls what my father showed me." She led them away from the water's edge. The girls trooped after her in single file, marching farther into the woods to the lush meadow Sherry had discovered with Lynn earlier in the day.

A sprinkling of flowers tucked their heads between the thick grass, hidden from an untrained eye.

"This is a blue monkshood," Sherry said, crouching down close to a foot-tall flower with lobed, toothed leaves and a thin stalk. Eagerly the girls gathered around the stringy plant that bloomed in blue and violet hues.

"The blue monkshood can grow as tall as seven feet," Sherry added.

"That's even bigger than Mr. Roarke," Diane said in awe.

At the sound of Jeff Roarke's name, Sherry's heart went still. She wished now that she'd taken time to talk to him and learn what he'd found so troubling. His eyes had seemed to avoid hers, and he'd been so...so distant. The minute they returned to camp, Sherry decided, she was going directly to his office. If she wasn't part of the problem, then she wanted to be part of the solution.

"Miss White?"

"Yes?" Shaking her head to clear her thoughts, Sherry smiled lamely.

"What's this?" Wendy pointed to a dwarf shrub with white blossoms and scalelike leaves that was close by.

"These are known as cassiopes." Sherry pronounced the name slowly and had the girls repeat it after her. "This is a hearty little flower. Some grow as far north as the arctic."

"How'd you learn so much about wildflowers?" Gretchen asked, her eyes wide and curious.

"Books, I bet," Diane shouted.

"Thank you, Miss White," Gretchen came back sarcastically.

"I did study books, but I learned far more by combining reading with taking hikes just like the one we're on today."

"Are there any other flowers here?"

"Look around you," Sherry answered, sweeping her arm in a wide arch. "They're everywhere."

"I wish Ralph were here," Pamela said with a loud sigh. "He likes the woods."

"What's this?" Sally asked, crouched down beside a yellow blossom.

"The western wallflower."

Gretchen giggled and called out, "Sally found a wallflower."

"It's better than being one," came the other girl's fiery retort.

"Girls, please!" Again Sherry found herself serving as referee to her young charges.

"I don't want camp to end," Wendy said suddenly, slumping to the ground. She shrugged out of her backpack and took out her Barbie and Ken dolls, holding them close. "But I want to go home, too."

"I feel the same way," Sherry admitted.

"You do?" Seven faces turned to study her.

"You bet. I love each one of you, and it's going to be hard to tell you all goodbye, but Camp Gitche Gumee isn't my home, and I miss my friends and my family." As much as she'd yearned to escape Phyliss, Sherry knew what she was saying was in fact, true. She did miss her father and her individualistic stepmother. And although California was beautiful, it wasn't Seattle.

"Are you planning to come back next year, Miss White?" Pam asked timidly.

Sherry nodded. "But only if you and Ralph will be here."

"I come back every summer," Gretchen said. "Next year I'm going to have my mother request you as my counselor."

Sherry tucked her arm around the little girl's shoulders and gently squeezed. "What about the lumpy mattress?"

"I said I was going to request you as my counselor, but I definitely don't want the same bed."

Sherry laughed at that, and so did the others.

The afternoon sped past, and by the time they returned to camp, Pam had gotten stung by a bee, Jan and Jill had suffered twin blisters on their right feet and Sally had happened upon two varieties of skipper moths. With a little help from her friends, she'd captured both and brought them back to camp to examine under her microscope.

The tired group of girls marched back into camp as heroes, as the other kids came running toward them, full of questions.

"Where did you guys go?"

"Will our counselor take us on a search for wildflowers, too?"

"How come you guys get to do all the fun stuff?"

"Miss White."

Jeff Roarke's voice reached Sherry, and with a wide, triumphant grin she turned to face him. The smile quickly faded at the cool reception in his gaze, and his dark, brooding look cut through her like a hot needle.

"You wanted to see me?" Sherry asked.

"That's correct." He motioned with his hand toward his office. "Lynn has agreed to take care of your girls until you return."

Lynn's smile was decidedly weak when Sherry's gaze sought out her friend's. Sherry paused, heaved in a deep breath and wiped the grime off the back of her neck with her hand. Her face felt hot and flushed. So much for her triumphant entry into Camp Gitche Gumee.

"Would you mind if I washed up first?" she asked.

Roarke hesitated.

"All right. A drink of water should do me."

They paused beside the water fountain, and Sherry took a long, slow drink, killing time. She straightened and wiped the clear water from her mouth. Again, Roarke's gaze didn't meet hers.

"I-it's about the references, isn't it?" she asked, trying her best to keep her voice from trembling. "I know I shouldn't have falsified them—I knew it was wrong—but I wanted this job so badly and—"

It didn't seem possible that Roarke's harsh features could tighten any more without hardening into granite. Yet, they did, right before her eyes.

"Roarke," she whispered.

"So you lied on the application, too."

Sherry's mind refused to cooperate. "Too? What do you mean, too? That's the only time I ever have, and I didn't consider it a real lie—I misled you is all."

His look seared her. "I suppose you 'misled' me in more than one area."

"Roarke, no...never." Sherry could see two months of a promising relationship evaporating into thin, stale air, and she was helpless to change it. She opened her mouth to defend herself and saw how useless it would be.

"Are you finished?" Roarke asked.

Feeling sick to her stomach, Sherry nodded.

"This way. There are people waiting to see you."

"People?"

At precisely that moment the door to Roarke's office opened and Phyliss came down the first step. With a wild, excited cry, she threw her arms in the air and cried, "Sherry, baby, I've found you at last."

Before Sherry had time to blink, she found herself clenched in her stepmother's arms in a grip that would have crushed anyone else. "Oh, darling, let me look at you." Gripping Sherry's shoulders, the older woman stepped back and sighed. "I've had every detective agency from here to San Francisco looking for you." She paused and laughed, the sound high and shrill. "I've got so much to tell you. Do you like my new hairstyle?" She paused and patted the side of her head. "Purple highlights—it drives your father wild."

Despite everything, Sherry laughed and hugged her. Loony, magnificent Phyliss. She'd never change.

"Your father is waiting to talk to you, darling. Do you have any idea what a wild-goose chase you've led us on? Never mind that now...we've had a marvelous time searching for you. This is something you may want to consider doing every summer. Your father and I have had a second honeymoon traveling all over the country trying to find you." She paused and laughed. "Sherry, sweetheart," she whispered, "before we leave, you and I must have a girl-to-girl talk about the camp director, Mr. Roarke. Why, he's handsome enough to stir up the blood of any woman. Now don't try to tell me you haven't noticed. I know better."

Flustered, Sherry looked up to find Roarke watching them both, obviously displeased.

Chapter Twelve

Roarke, please try to understand," Sherry pleaded.

A triumphant Phyliss and Virgil White had left Camp Gitche Gumee only minutes before. Her stepmother had evidently decided to look upon Sherry's disappearance as a fun game and had spent weeks tracking her down. It was as if Phyliss had won this comical version of hide-and-seek and could now return home giddy with jubilation for having outsmarted her stepdaughter.

As if that wasn't enough, Phyliss stayed long enough to inspect the camp kitchen and insist that Sherry tint her dark hair purple the minute she returned to Seattle—it was absolutely the in thing. She also enumerated in embarrassing detail Sherry's "many fine qualities" in front of Roarke, then paused demurely to flutter her lashes and announce that she'd die for a stepson-in-law as handsome as he was.

Sherry was convinced the entire camp sighed with relief the minute Phyliss and her father headed toward the exit in their powder-pink Cadillac. As they drove through the campgrounds, Phyliss leaned over her husband and blasted the horn in sharp toots, waving and generously blowing kisses as they went.

During the uncomfortable two hours that her parents were visiting, Sherry noted that Roarke didn't so much as utter a word to her. He carried on a polite conversation with her father, but Sherry had been too busy keeping Phyliss out of mischief to worry about what her father was telling Roarke.

Now that her parents were on their way back to Seattle, Sherry was free to speak to the somber camp director. She followed him back to his office, holding her tongue until he was seated behind the large desk that dominated his room.

"Now that you've met Phyliss you can understand why I needed to get away. I love her...in fact, I think she's wonderful, but all that mothering was giving me claustrophobia."

Roarke's smile was involuntary. "I must admit she's quite an individual."

Without invitation, Sherry pulled a chair close to Roarke's desk and sat down. She crossed her legs and leaned forward. "I-I'm sorry about the references on the application."

"You lied." His voice was a monotone, offering her little hope.

"I—I prefer to think of it as misleading you, and then only because it was necessary."

"Did you or did you not falsify your references?"

"Well, I did have the good references, I just equivocated a little on the addresses...."

"Then you were dishonest. A lie is a lie, so don't try to pretty it up with excuses."

Sherry swallowed uncomfortably. "Then I lied. But you wouldn't have known," she added quickly, before losing her nerve. "I mean, just now, today, when I mentioned it, you looked shocked. You didn't know until I told you."

"I knew." That wasn't completely true, Roarke thought. He'd suspected when the post office returned the first reference and then two of the others; but rather than investigate, Roarke had chosen to ignore the obvious for fear he'd be forced to fire her. Almost from the first week, he'd been so strongly attracted to her that he'd gone against all his instincts. Now he felt like a fool.

Sherry's hands trembled as she draped a thick strand of hair around her ear. She boldly met his gaze. "There are only a few days of camp left. Are . . . are you going to fire me?"

Roarke mulled over the question. He should. If any of the other counselors were to discover her deception, he would be made to look like a love-crazed fool.

"No," he answered finally.

In grateful relief Sherry momentarily closed her eyes.

"You understand, of course, that you won't be invited back as a counselor next summer."

His words burned through her like a hot poker. In one flat statement he was saying so much more. In effect, he was cutting her out of his life, severing her from his emotions and his heart. The tight knot that formed in her throat made it difficult to speak. "I understand," she said in a voice that was hardly more than a whisper. "I understand perfectly."

Sherry made her way to her cabin trapped in a haze of emotional pain. Lynn's words at the beginning of the camp session about Roarke's placing high regard on honesty returned to taunt her. The night they'd sat by the lake under the stars and kissed brought with it such a flood of memories that Sherry brushed the moisture from her cheek and sucked in huge breaths to keep from weeping.

"Miss White," Gretchen shouted when Sherry entered the cabin. "I liked your stepmother."

"Me, too," Jan added.

"Me, three," Jill said, and the twins giggled.

Sherry's smile was decidedly flat, although she did make the effort.

"She's so much fun!" Wendy held up her index finger to display a five-carat smoky topaz ring.

Costume jewelry, of course, Sherry mused. Phyliss didn't believe in real jewels, except her wedding ring.

"Phyliss told me I could have the ring," Wendy continued, "because anyone who appreciated Barbie and Ken the way I did deserved something special."

"She gave me a silk scarf," Diane said with a sigh. "She suggested I read Stephen King."

"Is her hair really purple?"

"She's funny."

Sherry sat at the foot of the closest bunk. "She's wonderful and fun and I love her."

"Do you think she'll visit next year?"

"I . . . I can't say." Another fib, Sherry realized. Phyliss wouldn't be coming to Camp Gitche Gumee because Sherry wouldn't be back.

"She sure is neat."

"Yes," Sherry said, and for the first time since she'd spoken to Roarke, the smile reached her eyes. "Phyliss is some kind of special."

"Miss White, Miss White, give me a hug," Sally cried, her suitcase in her hand. Sally was the first girl from Sherry's cabin to leave the camp. Camp Gitche Gumee had been dismissed at breakfast that morning. The bus to transport the youngsters to the airport was parked outside the dining room, waiting for the first group.

"Oh, Sally," Sherry said, wrapping her arms around the little girl and squeezing her tight. "I'm going to miss you so much."

"I had a whole lot of fun," she whispered, tears in her eyes. "More than at any other camp ever."

Tenderly, Sherry brushed the hair from Sally's forehead. "I did, too, sweetheart."

Goodbyes were difficult enough, but knowing that it was unlikely she would ever see her young charges again produced an even tighter pain within Sherry. She'd grown to love her girls, and the end of camp was all part of this bittersweet summer.

"Miss White," Gretchen cried, racing out of the cabin. "Miss White, guess what?"

Wendy followed quickly on Gretchen's heels. "I want to tell her," the other girl cried. "Gretchen, let me tell her."

A triumphant Wendy stormed to Sherry's side like an unexpected summer squall. "Look!" she declared breathlessly and held up the missing Ken-Richie.

"Where was he?" Sherry cried. The entire cabin had been searching for Ken-Richie for weeks.

"Guess," Gretchen said, hands placed on her hips. She couldn't hold her stern look long, and quickly dissolved into happy giggles. "I was sleeping on him."

Sherry's eyes rounded with shock. "You were sleeping on him?"

"I kept telling everyone how lumpy my mattress was, but no one would listen."

"Little wonder," Wendy said. "You complain about everything."

"Ever hear the story of the boy who cried wolf?" Sally asked.

"Of course, I know that story. I read it when I was three years old," Gretchen answered heatedly.

"But how'd Ken-Richie get under Gretchen's mattress?" Sherry wanted to know.

Wendy shuffled her feet back and forth and found the thick grass of utmost interest. "Well, actually," she mumbled, "I may have put him there for safekeeping."

"You?" Sherry cried.

"I forgot."

A pregnant pause followed Wendy's words before all four burst into helpless peals of laughter. It felt so good to laugh, Sherry decided. The past few days had been a living nightmare. In all that time, she hadn't spoken to Roarke once. He hadn't come to her. Hadn't so much as glanced in her direction. It was as though she were no longer a part of this camp, and he had effectively divorced her from his life.

Past experience in dealing with Roarke had taught Sherry to be patient and let his anger defuse itself before she approached him. However, time was running out; she was scheduled to leave camp the following day.

"The bus is ready," Sally said, and her voice sagged with regret. She hugged Sherry's middle one last time, then climbed into the van, taking a window seat. "Goodbye, Miss White," she cried, pressing her face against the glass. "Can I write you?"

"I'll answer every letter, I promise."

Sherry stood in the driveway until the van was out of sight, feeling more distressed by the moment. When she turned to go back to her cabin, she found Fred Spencer standing behind her. She stopped just short of colliding with his chest.

He frowned at her in the way she found so irritating.

"One down and six to go," she said, making polite conversation.

"Two down," he murmured, and turned to leave.

"Fred?" She stopped him.

"Yes?"

She held out her hand in the age-old gesture of friendship. "I enjoyed working with you this summer."

He looked astonished, but quickly took her hand and shook it enthusiastically. "You certainly added zip to this year's session."

She smiled, unsure how to take his comment.

"I hope you don't think my objections were anything personal," the older man added self-consciously. "I didn't think a lot of what you suggested would work, but you proved me wrong." His gaze shifted, then returned to her. "I hope you come back next summer, Miss White. I mean that."

Fred Spencer was the last person she'd ever expected to hear that from. "Thank you."

He tipped his hand to his hat and saluted her. "Have a good year."

"You, too."

But without Roarke, nothing would be good.

By three that afternoon, Sherry's cabin was empty. All her wizards were safely on their way back to their families. The log cabin that had only hours before been the focal point of laughter, tears and constant chatter seemed hollow without the sound of the seven little girls.

Aimlessly, Sherry wandered from one bunk to another, experiencing all the symptoms of the empty-nest syndrome. With nothing left to do, she went into her room and pulled out her suitcase. Feeling dejected and depressed, she laid it open on top of her mattress and sighed. She opened her drawer, but left it dangling as she slumped onto the end of the bed and reread the book the girls had written for her as a going-away present. Tenderly, her heart throbbing with love, she flipped through each page of the fairy tale created in her honor.

The girls had titled it *Sherry White and the Seven Wizards*. Each girl had developed a part of the story, drawn the pictures and created such a humorous scenario of life at Camp Gitche Gumee that even after she'd read it no less than ten times, the plot continued to make her laugh. And cry. She was going to miss her darling wizards. But no more than she would miss Roarke.

A polite knock at the front of the cabin caught Sherry by surprise. She set the book aside and stood.

"Yes." Her heart shot to her throat and rebounded against her ribs at the sight of Jeff Roarke framed in the open doorway of the cabin.

"Miss White."

He knew how she detested his saying her name in such a cool, distant voice, she thought. He was saying it as a reminder of how far apart they were now, telling her in two words that she'd committed the unforgivable sin and nothing could be the same between them again.

"Mr. Roarke," she returned, echoing his frigid tone.

Roarke's mouth tightened into a thin, impatient line.

"Listen," she said, trying again. "I understand and fully agree with you."

"You do?" His brows came together in a puzzled frown. "Agree with me about what?"

"Not having me back next year. What I did was stupid and foolish and I'll never regret anything more in my life." Her actions had cost her Roarke's love. Because there was nothing else for her to do, Sherry would leave Camp Gitche Gumee and would wonder all her life if she'd love another man with the same intensity that she loved Jeff Roarke.

"Fred told me the two of you had come to terms."

Sherry rubbed her palms together. Fred had smiled at her for the first time all summer. Sherry could afford to be generous with him.

"He isn't so bad," she murmured softly.

"Funny, that's what he said about you."

Sherry attempted a smile, but the effort was feeble and wobbly at best.

With his hands buried deep within his pockets, Roarke walked into the cabin and strolled around the room. The silence hung heavy between them. Abruptly, he turned to face her. "So you feel I made the right decision not to ask you back."

She didn't know why he insisted on putting her through this. "I understand that I didn't give you much of a choice."

"What if I made another request of you?"

Sherry's gaze held his, daring to hope, daring to believe that he would love her enough to overcome her deception. "Another request?"

"Yes." In an uncustomary display of nervousness, Roarke rifled his fingers through his hair, mussing the well-groomed effect. "It might be better if I elaborate a little."

"Please." Sherry continued to hold herself stiff.

"Camp Gitche Gumee is my brainchild."

Sherry already knew that, but she didn't want to interrupt him.

"As a youngster I was like many of these children. I was too intelligent to fit in comfortably with my peers and too immature to be accepted into the adult community."

Sherry just nodded.

"The camp was born with the desire to offer a summer program for such children. I regretted having hired you the first week of camp, but I quickly changed my mind. Maybe because I've never experienced the kind of fun you introduced to your girls, I tended to be skeptical of your methods." He paused and exhaled sharply. So many things were rummaging around in his head. He didn't know if he was saying too much or not enough.

"I'm not sure I understand," Sherry said.

"I'd like you to come back."

"As a counselor?"

"No." He watched the joy drain from her eyes and tasted her disappointment. "Actually I was hoping that you'd consider becoming my partner."

"Your partner?" Sherry didn't understand.

Silently, Roarke was cursing himself with every swear word he knew. He was fumbling this badly. For all his intelligence he should be able to tell a woman he loved her and wanted her to share his life. He rubbed his hand along the back of his neck and exhaled again. None of the things he longed to tell her were coming out right. "I'm doing this all wrong."

"Doing what? Roarke," she said. "You want me to be your partner—then fine. I'd do anything to come back to Camp Gitche Gumee. Work in the kitchen. Be a housekeeper. Even garden. All I want in the world is here."

"I'm asking you to be my partner for more reasons than you know. The children love you. In a few weeks' time, you've managed to show everyone in the camp, including me and Fred Spencer, that learning can be fun. There wasn't a camper here who doesn't want you back next year."

"As your partner what would be my responsibilities?"

"You'd share the management of the camp with me and plan curriculum and the other activities that you've instigated this summer."

Some of the hope that had been building inside her died a silent death. "I see. I'd consider it an honor to return in any capacity."

"There is one problem, however."

"Yes?"

"The director's quarters is only a small cabin."

"I understand." Naturally, he'd want his quarters.

Roarke closed his eyes to the mounting frustration. He couldn't have done a worse job of this had he tried. Finally he just blurted it out. "Sherry, I'm asking you to marry me."

Joy crowded her features. "Yes," she cried, zooming to her feet. Her acceptance was followed by an instantaneous flood of tears.

"Damn it, now I've made you cry."

"Can't you tell when a woman is so overcome with happiness that she can't contain herself?" She wiped the moisture from her cheeks in a furious action. "Why are you standing over there? Why aren't you right here, kissing me and holding me?" She paused and challenged him, almost afraid of his answer. "Jeff Roarke, do you love me?"

"Dear God, yes."

They met halfway across the floor. Roarke reached for her and hauled her into his arms, burying his face in the gentle slope of her neck and shoulder while he drew in several calming breaths, feeling physically and mentally exhausted. He'd never messed anything up more in his life. This woman had to love him. She must, to have allowed him to put her through that.

Being crushed against him as she was made speaking impossible. Not that Sherry minded. Her brain was so fuddled and her throat so thick with emotion that she probably wouldn't have made sense anyway.

Roarke tucked his index finger beneath her chin and raised her mouth to meet his. His hungry kiss rocked her to the core of her being. Countless times, his mouth feasted on hers, as though it were impossible to get enough of her. Not touching her all these weeks had been next to impossible, and now, knowing that she felt for him the same things he did for her made the ache of longing all the more intense.

Freely, Sherry's hands roved his back, reveling in the muscular feel of his skin beneath her fingers. All the while, Roarke's mouth made moist forays over her lips, dipping again and again to sample her sweet kiss.

"Oh, love," he whispered, lackadaisically sliding his mouth back and forth over her lips. "I can't believe this is happening." He ground his hips against her softness and sharply sucked in his breath. "Nothing can get more real than this."

"Nothing," she agreed and trapped his head between her two hands in an effort to study him. "Why?"

"Why do I love you?"

Her smile went soft. "No, how can you love me after what I did?"

"I met Phyliss, remember?"

"But . . ."

"But it took me a few days to remember that you'd tried to tell me about the references."

"I did?"

Resisting her was impossible, and he kissed the tip of her pert nose. "Yes. The night at the lake. Remember? I knew then, or strongly suspected, but I didn't want to hear it, didn't want to face the truth because that would have demanded some response. Yet even when I was forced to look at the truth, I couldn't send you away. Doing that would have been like sentencing my own heart to solitary confinement for life."

"Oh, Roarke." She leaned against him, linking her hands at the base of his spine. "I do love you."

"I know."

Abruptly, her head came up. "What about school?"

"What about it?"

"I've only got one year left."

"I wouldn't dream of having you drop out," he rushed to assure her. "You can transfer your credits and finish here in California."

Sherry pressed her head against his heart and sighed expressively. "I may give up school for a year or two and go back later."

"But why? There's no reason for you to delay your education because of marriage."

Lifting her head, Sherry pressed her finger over his lips. "I want a baby, Roarke. Your baby."

Roarke met the intensity of her gaze with all the deep desire of his own. He wanted Sherry to share his life. She was marvelous with the youngsters, and having her work with him at Camp Gitche Gumee would be an advantage to the camp and the children. But with all of his plans, he hadn't paused to think of their having a child of their own. The love he felt for her swelled within him until he felt weak with it. And strong, so strong that he seemed invincible.

"Someday we'll be sending our own wizards to this camp," Sherry told him.

Roarke's hold on her tightened.

"The girls told me you were my prince," she said, her gaze falling on the book her wizards had created.

"We're going to be so happy, Sherry, my love."

"Forever and ever," she agreed, just as the book said.

* * * * *

Silhouette ❦ Romance

COMING NEXT MONTH

#580 CALHOUN—Diana Palmer
Calhoun Ballenger had raised Abby Clark since childhood, but now that she was twenty-one, she'd set his heart on fire... and was determined to make this long, tall Texan her own! The first book of Diana Palmer's LONG, TALL TEXANS trilogy!

#581 THE SCORPIO MAN—Sara Grant
Melissa Wyatt came to Elba for underwater photography—not for a romance with some mysterious playboy. So what if Nico Giordano's eyes were as green and deep as the sea? She wasn't about to be stung by a Scorpio man.

#582 WORDS OF LOVE—Octavia Street
Was devastatingly attractive Christopher Fields a spy, a gunrunner or a Secret Service man? Annie White didn't know, but there was no defense against his words of love....

#583 AN INDEPENDENT LADY—Roslyn McDonald
Dirk Warner had hired aloof architect Terry Lovell to restore his antebellum house, but suddenly he had plans of his own to make a house into a home. Would his love restore Terry's broken heart?

#584 RAINDANCE AUTUMN—Phyllis Halldorson
Reserved Annelise Kelsey was looking for love with a city slicker. Could a rugged country man like Rusty Watt convince her he was just the shining knight she'd been waiting for?

#585 MOON IN THE WATER—Victoria Glenn
Jacob Van Cleef wouldn't tolerate anyone challenging his authority over the small town of Half Moon Falls—until fiery Liza Langley breezed into town and poked her pretty nose into his business....

AVAILABLE THIS MONTH:

#574 WORTH THE RISK
Brittany Young

#575 SARAH'S CHOICE
Karen Young

#576 THE FOREVER MAN
Theresa Weir

#577 THE TIDES OF LOVE
Elizabeth Hunter

#578 A DELICATE BALANCE
Arlene James

#589 ALMOST PARADISE
Book 3 of the LEGENDARY
LOVERS TRILOGY.
Debbie Macomber

ATTRACTIVE, SPACE SAVING BOOK RACK

Display your most prized novels on this handsome and sturdy book rack. The hand-rubbed walnut finish will blend into your library decor with quiet elegance, providing a practical organizer for your favorite hard-or soft-covered books.

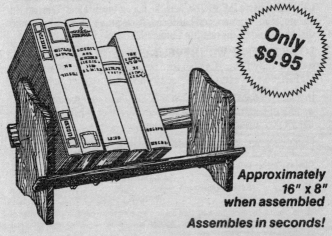

Only $9.95

Approximately 16" x 8" when assembled

Assembles in seconds!

To order, rush your name, address and zip code, along with a check or money order for $10.70* ($9.95 plus 75¢ postage and handling) payable to *Silhouette Books*.

Silhouette Books
Book Rack Offer
901 Fuhrmann Blvd.
P.O. Box 1396
Buffalo, NY 14269-1396

Offer not available in Canada.

BKR-2A

*New York and Iowa residents add appropriate sales tax.